Acclaim For the Work of
MAX ALLAN COLLINS!

"Crime fiction aficionados are in for a treat…a neo-pulp noir classic."
— *Chicago Tribune*

"No one can twist you through a maze with as much intensity and suspense as Max Allan Collins."
— *Clive Cussler*

"Collins never misses a beat…All the stand-up pleasures of dime-store pulp with a beguiling level of complexity."
— *Booklist*

"Collins has an outwardly artless style that conceals a great deal of art."
— *New York Times Book Review*

"Max Allan Collins is the closest thing we have to a 21st-century Mickey Spillane and…will please any fan of old-school, hardboiled crime fiction."
— *This Week*

"A suspenseful, wild night's ride [from] one of the finest writers of crime fiction that the U.S. has produced."
— *Book Reporter*

"This book is about as perfect a page turner as you'll

D1019879

"Father," I said.

The priest turned and looked at me. He got a little smile going and nodded and looked away.

Oh, he was nobody's dummy this one, a real college graduate. He was well aware that his role as priest called for acknowledging the respects of the faithful. Brother.

"Father," I said, and I let him see I was wearing gloves in August. His eyes figured it out.

"Oh God," he said. Prayer-soft.

"Let's go to the can."

"Oh God."

"All I want's what you have. Nothing else is going to happen."

"Oh God."

"Stay calm, now, don't say anything...okay. Okay. You settled down?"

He shivered once. Then he nodded.

"Okay," I said. "We'll walk to the can and we'll talk about it. Now get up. Now."

He stood and I stood and I took his arm. We walked in front of the young couple and I said excuse me and smiled and they smiled back. I ushered him down the hall of empty offices and into the can.

I locked the door...

HARD CASE CRIME BOOKS
BY MAX ALLAN COLLINS:

QUARRY
QUARRY'S LIST
QUARRY'S DEAL
QUARRY'S CUT
QUARRY'S VOTE
THE LAST QUARRY
THE FIRST QUARRY
QUARRY IN THE MIDDLE
QUARRY'S EX
THE WRONG QUARRY
QUARRY'S CHOICE
QUARRY IN THE BLACK

DEADLY BELOVED
SEDUCTION OF THE INNOCENT
TWO FOR THE MONEY

DEAD STREET *(with Mickey Spillane)*
THE CONSUMMATA *(with Mickey Spillane)*

QUARRY

by **Max Allan Collins**

A HARD CASE CRIME NOVEL

A HARD CASE CRIME BOOK

(HCC-S02)

First Hard Case Crime edition: October 2015

Published by

Titan Books
A division of Titan Publishing Group Ltd
144 Southwark Street
London SE1 0UP

in collaboration with Winterfall LLC

Print edition ISBN 978-1-78565-067-3
E-book ISBN 978-1-78329-884-6

Design direction by Max Phillips
www.maxphillips.net

Typeset by Swordsmith Productions

Printed in the United States of America

Visit us on the web at www.HardCaseCrime.com

To Donald E. Westlake
thanks for writing

"Violence is as American as cherry pie."
H. RAP BROWN

"I had gotten a taste of death and found it palatable to the extent that I could never again eat the fruits of a normal civilization."
MICKEY SPILLANE

QUARRY

I

I closed my eyes and saw the face of the man I would kill. Back at the Howard Johnson's, in the restroom, the Broker had showed me the photograph and asked me if I wanted to take it with me; I said no, just let me look at it for a minute. Now, ten minutes later, I thought of the face: a soft fleshy oval with a fat Jewish nose sticking out of it.

I opened my eyes and saw the complex of brown brick buildings up ahead. The main building was a pair of long two-stories that joined a central tower. From where I was walking I could just make out the words "Quad City Airport" on the tower. The afternoon was just trailing into dusk and they hadn't turned on the lights yet.

Before I'd started across the grassy field between the Howard Johnson's and the airport, the group of buildings with the several hangars looked good-size, no O'Hare, but good-size. By the time I approached the parking lot, the place looked smaller, as if I'd been walking toward a scale model. Tiny gardens of red and white and purple flowers were stuck here and there around the parking lot, lip service paid to nature in the midst of bricks and cement and jet fumes. The flowers didn't belong here, and neither did I; I wanted to be in a T-shirt instead of a suit, and I wanted to be relaxing in the sun somewhere instead of on a job.

Especially this job, this pain-in-the-ass job.

Going in I almost got my briefcase knocked out of my hand as two guys in dark suits came rushing out the front door like their luggage had bombs inside and they were the Bomb Squad. Which was airport-typical: half the people in a hurry rushing around acting important; half the people in no hurry strolling around acting important. Assholes.

Inside was wine-color marble and blue-green plaster. There was a sweep to the way the building was put together that probably seemed futuristic in 1950. Now it was a fucking dinosaur. Like that elevator stuck in the middle of everything, housed in a cylinder with a staircase curved around, the cylinder covered in garish red plastic that had bubbled in places.

The first thing I did was check the downstairs cans. They were all pretty big (four stalls—three pay and a free) but even with the airport in a kind of lull right now, it was clear none of them would do. Then I climbed the staircase that circled the elevator and before I got started in on the upstairs cans, I saw him.

There was a priest and a young couple in their twenties and a soldier and a sailor and two old ladies and a businessman, all sitting around the indoor observation deck on the black-cushioned seats, looking out the big picture window at the runway. He was the priest.

All in black, of course, except for the white clerical collar. And a gray putty face, gray except for where some burst veins roadmapped his nose. He was wearing a black toupee that looked like one. He had on dark sunglasses.

A priest. With that Jewish nose and sunglasses at dusk, no less, he's going to pass for a priest. With some guys you might just as well stand to the side and wait for them to kill themselves, they're that stupid.

He didn't catch me looking at him so I went on ahead and checked out the cans on this floor. I took in both halls that branched off the central tower building and found a can apiece and a lot of empty offices. One hall had activity in the end office, so I settled for the can down the other, completely deserted hall. That was fine because it was the best in the building, the other one on this floor being like the downstairs johns, big and designed with airport cattle in mind. Mine was for the paid help, with a single free one-seater but lots of room to stand and smoke. Also, every other can in the airport had a push door with no lock; this one had a firmly closing door with locking knob.

I went back downstairs without even glancing at the priest. I walked to the Hertz desk and asked the pretty blonde who did I see about luggage lockers. She said they're just around the corner, sir, and I said, no, who's in charge of them. She smiled and picked up her phone and dialed and a moment later a young guy in a blue blazer asked if he could help and I told him what I wanted and he said fine and took some money from me. We went to where two walls of bright steel luggage lockers faced each other tight and I put my briefcase in one of the compartments and he marked down the locker number and asked for a name and I gave him one. He said thanks and I said thanks and he went away.

With him gone, I reopened the locker, snapped the briefcase open and got out the pair of gray gloves and slipped them on. From the briefcase I took my folded raincoat, which I draped over my arm, and the nine-millimeter silenced automatic, which I gripped in my right hand, the draped raincoat covering my whole right forearm and hand. I shut the briefcase and sealed it back up in the locker.

Upstairs I walked over to the priest and sat next to him. He was looking out at the big silver jet, a 737 trimmed in United Airlines red-white-and-blue. The sky was slate-color with big brushstrokes of orange cloud. I wondered if he could see all that in those goddamn sunglasses.

"Father," I said.

The priest turned and looked at me. He got a little smile going and nodded and looked away.

Oh, he was nobody's dummy this one, a real college graduate. He was well aware that his role as priest called for acknowledging the respects of the faithful. Brother.

"Father," I said, and I let him see I was wearing gloves in August. His eyes figured it out.

"Oh God," he said. Prayer-soft.

"Let's go to the can."

"Oh God."

"All I want's what you have. Nothing else is going to happen."

"Oh God."

"Stay calm, now, don't say anything...okay. Okay. You settled down?"

He shivered once. Then he nodded.

"Okay," I said. "We'll walk to the can and we'll talk about it. Now get up. Now."

He stood and I stood and I took his arm. We walked in front of the young couple and I said excuse me and smiled and they smiled back. I ushered him down the hall of empty offices and into the can.

I locked the door.

He ran ahead and opened up the stall and puked in the stool, with the speed and ease of a runner passing a baton in a relay.

When he was through, I said, "Flush it and come out here."

He did.

The whole damn room stank, now. Like the job itself stank. All I could think was, this isn't what I do, this isn't my style. What am I, some kind of shakedown artist? That goddamn Broker's going to pay for this breach of contract. I work a certain kind of job, and shit like this isn't part of it.

I said, "Where?"

He was shaking; his cheeks were trying to crawl off his face.

I repeated myself.

He said nothing. He did nothing. He looked at me out of glazed eyes and just stood there.

"Look," I said. "Nobody's going to do anything to you

if you're sensible. You took something from some people and they want it back. Return what you took, and you can catch your plane as long as from now on you stay away from these people and theirs. It's that simple. Hell, you'll just be out a job you're out anyway."

He said, "Please."

"Stay cool, now. Look at it this way: you're in possession of a valuable commodity. Hand that commodity over to me and you can walk out of here. An even swap."

He patted his cheeks and tried to coax them to stay. His face over the clerical collar turned from ash gray to reddish gray. He was thinking about crying.

Shit.

"Look," I said, "I don't like to hurt people. I'm not into that at all. Why don't you just cooperate?"

"It's in my baggage."

"I don't believe you."

"I tell you it's in my baggage."

"I don't believe you, I don't believe you'd let this off your person."

"I don't care what you believe, it's in my baggage, I checked my baggage already and it's already been taken out to the plane."

"If you're telling the truth…"

"I am!"

"If you're telling the truth, get out your rosary."

"You said…"

"I said I'm not into hurting people. I'm not. It won't hurt, Father, it'll just be black. All of a sudden. Real black."

"But, please, please, listen to me, I checked the bags...
the stuff's in my bags and that's the truth, I'm sorry, Christ
knows I'd give it to you and be done but I'm sorry."

I let the automatic peek out from under the draped
raincoat. "Is that still the truth?"

He closed his eyes and shook his head no.

"Where?" I said.

He started to take off his coat.

I brought the gun up and said, "Watch it, Father!"

"No, no! Wait!" He eased out of the coat and handed it
toward me. Offered it. "It's the coat. The lining. In the
lining."

"Get it out of the lining."

"You, you said you'd let me catch my plane. I'm gonna
miss my plane."

"Maybe. Get it out of the lining."

"It's sewn in, uh, under, I mean..."

"Rip it out."

He did. He tugged free the lining and reached inside
the gutted coat and pulled out two plastic bags, stapled at
their tops, a lump of white powder in each.

Inside my head, I shit my pants.

Okay, Broker. Is this what you got me into? Okay. He
gave me the bags and I slipped them in my suitcoat pocket.

"What now?" he said.

"Throw that lining away," I said.

He balled it up and shoved it into the canister for used
paper towels. I motioned to him to put the coat back on
and he did.

"Well?" he said.

"You can go," I said. "But not till I'm gone. I'm going to have to knock you out."

"My, my plane! You said...but now I'll miss my plane..."

"You're under the gun and you worry about your plane. Christ. Just be thankful you're getting out of this with your ass in one piece."

"Please, I'll wait in here, I can wait ten minutes and still make it."

I rubbed my chin. "Suppose I could tie you up and by the time you got loose I'd be gone..."

"Sure, sure, you could do that! Here, I'll untie my shoelaces, you can use that to tie me."

"No, never mind," I said. "I got some rope in my pocket."

"Oh. Oh well, fine."

"First you get in that stall there."

"In there?"

"In there."

"It stinks in there."

"That's because you puked." Christ, this guy.

He opened the stall.

"Put the seat down," I said.

He did.

"Now sit." He did.

"Put your hands together."

As he was doing that, I shot him in the chest.

2

The water was all around me and cold. I bobbed back up to the surface, grabbed a breath, and breast-stroked over to the side of the pool, pulled myself up and out, and then went to the board and dove back in.

Five minutes later I stood in the shallow and the water lapped up against my thighs and I heard a voice say, "So here you are."

I looked up and she was in a black bikini. She was very tan, brown-black tan, and she was slender, with hardly any breasts and a ribby rib cage but if she'd been facing the other way I would've been reminded what a fine round little ass she had.

"Didn't think I'd be seeing you again," she said, "didn't think you'd still be around."

"Come on in," I said.

"No. You come out. I'm not getting my hair wet, I just want some air."

I climbed out and went after my towel. When I was dry I looked around and saw she'd taken a lounge chair well back from the pool's edge to keep her from getting wet if some clown like me dove in. She leaned back, her longish black hair hanging away from her face, and it was like she was sunbathing only she was just sitting there staring up at the clouds and the moon. I joined her, pulling up another lounge chair and sitting.

"I fell asleep," she said.

"You were asleep when I left," I said.

"Were you coming back?"

"Sure."

"I didn't figure on seeing you. I thought it was hit and run."

"No. I slept there with you a little, then came out for a swim."

"Where'd you change?"

"Went up to my room for my trunks. When's your husband going to be back?"

"Not till late. He'll be interviewing all evening."

I didn't say anything for a while. I was trying to remember her name. Helen, I think she said it was.

"How's the water?" she said.

"Cold. Fine."

"You refreshed?"

"Sure. You rested up?"

"Sure. Want to go in and fuck?"

"Why not?"

I followed her from the swimming area across some grass to the little cement patio to her room and then in the sliding glass doors. My room was up on the second floor and didn't have such convenient pool access. She slid shut the window-door behind us and drew the curtain. She undid the bikini bra-top and let it drop; her breasts were small and her nipples large and dark, so

with all that tan only a small circle of white separated
dark texture from dark. It was a sexy effect. She lowered
her bikini bottoms and she was dark and hairy down
there against white skin. All this made up for her skinni-
ness. I got my trunks off and we lay on the bed.

She was all technique and no passion, like she lost that
part of it somewhere along the line and spent lots of time
since looking for it. She told me her husband hired people
for industry and went around interviewing applicants all
the time and when he discovered she was cheating while
he was off on business, he started taking her along. The
husband always did his interviews at downtown hotels
wherever they happened to be, but she insisted that they
stay at motels so she could be near pool and sunshine.
That was as far as her explanation went, but the rest was
obvious enough: while her husband interviewed at the
downtown hotel, she picked up traveling salesmen and
the like at the motel, mostly by sitting around the pool in
her black bikini.

I had got to the Howard Johnson's Motor Lodge about
an hour before I was supposed to meet the Broker in the
restaurant part, so I checked in and managed to get
picked up and laid by Helen or whatever-her-name-was
before I was due to confab with Broker. Well, I did end
up a little late but how was I to know the Broker had
something last-minute urgent on his mind. I mean, he
never pulled anything like that on me before.

And never again. I was glad I'd thought to arrange for
a month rental on one of those lockers at the airport.

I figured Broker might be putting me onto something big and maybe I'd want to cache some or all of whatever it was for myself. So one of the lockers, which was good for only two days, had one of the little plastic bags of white powder in it; and another locker, good for a whole month, had the other. And I had both keys and Broker by the balls.

Of course this thing with Helen or whoever had worked out pretty nice, since the bitch provided me an alibi of sorts, not that I'd use it. As far as she knew, I'd screwed her, slept a while, then gone out for a swim. She didn't know I stepped out to give last rites to a priest.

She sat up in bed, leaned back against the headboard and got a cigarette going. Her breasts were droopy and didn't look so sexy anymore and I saw she had some lines in her face and all of a sudden she looked like a middle-aged housewife who slept around a lot, which is what she was. After a while it occurred to her she ought to offer me a cigarette too, and I told her I didn't use them.

"Clean liver, huh?"

"That shit can kill you," I said, fanning her smoke out of my face. "But it's your life, do what you want."

"You like to play at being hard, don't you."

"You don't seem to mind me hard."

She grinned and reached a hand down and played with me but neither it nor I was having any.

So she gave up and a few seconds went by and she said, "I got some booze, you thirsty?"

I was thinking that one over when outside, sirens cut the air.

"What the hell was that?" she said.

"Sirens."

"Yeah, that's what I thought it was. Sounded like they went by here. Something happen at the airport, you suppose?"

"Somebody had a heart attack maybe."

"Yeah. Ambulance, then, not police."

"Who knows."

"Yeah. Hey, should I build us some drinks or not?"

"I don't think so."

"Come on."

"Look," I said, "this has been pleasant, but I got no desire to do a number with your husband should he come back early or something. I'll just put my trunks on and go swimming again, okay?"

"Aw, stick around."

"No thanks."

"Prick."

I shrugged and got my trunks on and slid the glass door open. I strolled out to the pool and walked over to the diving board. Up on the board I bounced and looked across the grassy field toward the airport. It was all lit up, but no more than usual, and I couldn't make out whether there were any ambulance or cop car lights up there. Not that it mattered. I dove in. The water was cold.

3

The best part of the meal was the skillet of mushrooms. The Chablis was okay, but I don't know enough about wine to tell good from bad. But I do know mushrooms, I've gone picking them before, and know enough to take the sponge and leave the button top be. You never can tell about button top, unless you get commercial grown. Like these were. Big and round as half dollars and plump and juicy and fine.

The steak was just fair, being grainy like maybe it was injected with something to make it tender while it was still a cow, but you got to remember too that I was full on bread and salad and mushrooms before I even got to the steak. Finishing the wine seemed a good top priority, and the last of it was just trickling down my throat when the Broker and his wife walked past my table, neither one of them showing a trace of recognition.

Which made sense with the wife, since she never saw me before. She was an aristocratic-looking, icy ice-blonde of maybe thirty-five who probably came out of one of those exclusive girl's schools with a name like a winter resort, where a nun or some other kind of old maid had taught her how to be a proper little glacier.

She was good-looking enough to make you wonder if

Broker picked her like he would any front or maybe there was some sex or love in it somewhere.

A girl in a short-skirted barmaid outfit seated the Broker and his missus in a secluded corner where two wine-rack walls met. She took their drink order and then a kid in a rust-color puffy-sleeve cavalier shirt waited on them. The outfits fitted in with the glorified old-English pub atmosphere of the place: high ceiling, rough wood, a central roaring fireplace (gas), and huge wrought-iron chandeliers above pouring out coppery semilight from candles (electric).

I poked at my steak and waited for Broker to make a move. He made an effort not to look my way. I stared at him. At his brown double-knit pinstripe suit. At his distinguished white hair. At the prissy expression under the wispy mustache.

He stood, excused himself with his wife, who didn't seem to notice he was getting up to go. He was a tall man, six-two and well-built, but he walked like he was gelded.

I watched him go past me and round the fireplace and head toward the restrooms. I waited a minute or two— I was willing to play his game that far—and then went after him.

He was washing his hands. A guy was taking a leak and one of the crappers was occupied. I walked over to one of the urinals and got busy.

After a while everybody left, except Broker and me, and I joined him at the sinks. Broker stopped washing his hands, but he kept the water running.

"Well?" he said.

"Don't ever try pulling anything like this on me again, Broker."

"How did it go?"

"It went."

"Did you get what he had?"

I looked at the Broker's double-knit brown suit. He was wearing a blue shirt and a white tie and his cheeks were rosy. He was fifty and he looked forty and his face was long and fleshy without many lines.

"I got it," I said.

Somebody came in and Broker started washing his hands again. I joined him. The guy did what he had to and left.

"Seems like when I work with you," I said, "all my time's spent in toilets."

"Is that where you took care of him? In a restroom?"

"No. I walked him out to the runway and threw him in front of a Boeing."

A little dark guy with a little dark son came in and stood at the urinals, like a big salt shaker and a smaller pepper. When they were done they seemed to want to wash their hands, but Broker and me had the sink concession, so the pair gave up quick and left.

"What are you upset about, Quarry?"

"Horse."

"What are you talking about?"

"I'm talking about H, Broker. Smack. Heroin, horse, shit, horseshit!"

"Will you please keep your voice down?"

"Christ, Broker. That's all I need is to get found with a bundle of that on me. I got enough fucking risk going for me as it is."

"You disappoint me, Quarry."

"I disappoint you."

"You were told your man had a valuable package which did not belong to him. You weren't told to examine the contents of the package."

"It was a lump of snow in a plastic bag, Broker, it didn't take a goddamn chemist to tell."

"Since when are you so God almighty precautious? You complain of risk. Yet you use the same gun from job to job, don't you? That would seem a dangerous habit to me."

"That is one thing. This other today is something else."

"I'm not going to stand here and argue with you, Quarry. My hands are getting puckered from washing."

"Your hands are getting puckered. My ass is getting puckered! Look, I work one kind of thing, and I work it one kind of way, you know that better than anyone else, but what do you do? You bring me in for a half-ass deal like this one."

"This was last minute, Quarry, I called you in for something else entirely, and…"

"I don't like getting brought to town for one job and doing another. I don't like playing courier with a load of H. You want to play with smack, get a pusher. And this humiliating people, I got no stomach for that. You got somebody who's going to die, fine, I'll be the means. You want strong-arm, get a goon."

"Are you quite finished?"

"Don't pull that pompous bullshit tone on me, Broker. I've known you too long. I know what you are."

"If you don't like working for me, Quarry, why don't you just quit?"

"What? What did you say?"

"I said if you don't like working for me you can always quit."

"Now that tears it. Now that really fucking tears it."

"What are you talking about?"

"*You* work for *me*, Broker, don't forget that…I work for you like Richard Burton works for his agent."

Broker sighed. "Where's the stuff, Quarry?"

"Never do this to me again, Broker. Understand? Nothing else like this. Or you're going to see the side of this business you don't like seeing."

"Where's the stuff?"

"Do you get my meaning, Broker?"

"Yes. Where's the stuff?"

"Where's my money?"

Broker turned off the faucet and wiped his hands on a paper towel. He took an envelope from his inside jacket pocket. He handed the envelope to me and I looked inside: three thousand in hundreds. I put the envelope in my inside pocket.

"I'm still at the Howard Johnson's," I said. "You come talk to me there. You know what room I'm in. I'm sick of using cans for my office."

"What?"

"And don't send anybody around to see me, Broker, or

I'll do bad things to them. You come. We got talking to do."

"Don't play with me, Quarry."

"Who's playing? Better zip up, Broker."

"Quarry..."

I dried my hands and left.

4

I suppose at this point I should be filling you in on my background and telling you how I got into such a specialized line of work. Don't count on it. There are two things you won't get from me and that's details about my past and my real name. The closest you'll get to a name is Quarry, which is an alias suggested by the Broker and I always kind of liked it, as aliases go. Or I did until I asked Broker why he suggested an offbeat name like that one and he chuckled and said, "Know what a quarry is, don't you? It's rock and it's hollowed out." Broker isn't known for his sense of humor.

I will sketch in some of my background, in case you feel the need to try to understand me. I'm a veteran of the Vietnam fuckup, which was where I learned about the meaninglessness of life and death, though the point wasn't really driven home until I arrived back in the states and found my wife shacked up with a guy named Williams who had a bungalow in La Mirada and a job in a garage. I was going to shoot the son of a bitch, but waited till I cooled down enough to think rationally. Then I went to his house where he was in his driveway on his back working under his car and kicked the jack out…once in a movie I heard death referred to as "the big crushout," and for that poor bastard the phrase couldn't have been more apropos. I didn't shoot my wife, or drop a car on her either. I just divorced her. Or rather she divorced me.

Of course no court in the world would have touched me, a cuckolded serviceman fresh home from the fight. But no one wanted me for an overnight house guest either. I couldn't find work, even though I was a fully qualified mechanic…and it wasn't like there weren't any openings. The garage where Williams worked could've used a man, that was for sure.

The only relative I had who would even look me in the face was my old man, who came out to L.A. to see me after I had my little marital problem. He told me not to come home, said I'd made my stepmother nervous even before I started murdering people and God only knew how I'd affect her now. I never did ask the old man which murders he was talking about, the dozen or so in Vietnam or the one in California.

Since I couldn't go home to Ohio with my father, I just hung around L.A. for a month or so, spending my money as fast as I could, going to movies during the days and bars at night. That got old fast. California got old fast. It was where I was stationed before going overseas and was where I fell into the star-crossed romance that ended in marriage, among other things, with that brown-haired bitch whose face is fuzzy in my memory now.

I don't know how the Broker got a line on me. Maybe it's like pro football teams recruiting players; maybe Broker sends scouts around to bars to look for guys with faces full of no morality. Or maybe Broker and his people pay attention to certain of us who get back from service and have problems. I know mine was in the papers and got enough publicity to keep me from getting jobs when I applied. You know I never did figure out how everybody could be so goddamn back-patting sympathetic and still not be willing to risk giving me a job.

Everybody but Broker. He had a job for me. I don't remember the conversation. I know it was elliptical. You don't come right out and ask somebody if he'd like to kill people for money. Even Uncle Sugar is more subtle than that.

Anyway, Broker showed up one day at what could best be described as my fleabag one-room apartment in L.A. and somehow or other got across to me what he was talking about...that I could make top dollar continuing to do what I had just finished doing for peanuts and, in one case, for free. Killing people, that is.

I accepted without hesitation. My eager but unemotional "yes" must've nearly scared the Broker off. He told me later he was usually wary of a fast yes; he didn't want anyone working with him who might be the type who drooled for a chance to shoot anything that breathed: madmen don't make the world's most reliable, efficient employees. But my lack of emotion counterbalanced any such fear Broker might've harbored, especially on top of the thorough researching he'd had done on me.

Why did I say yes? Why did I say yes so quickly? I guess I was hungry for the chance to do something, anything, especially a high-paying something or anything. Though I'd learned in Nam to accept life and death as meaning-less, I'd also learned the importance of survival. Maybe that's inconsistent, holding life and death void of meaning while valuing survival. All I know is it's how I think and feel and live, so I don't care.

I said I wouldn't go into detail and I won't. All I'll say is that by the time Broker called me to the Quad Cities and tossed that airport business in my lap, I'd been doing freelance work for him for five and a half years. And I did consider myself a free agent, even though I worked solely through Broker, since I had no doubt I could hook up with some other similar "booking agent" with no trouble. There were other Brokers around, though I didn't know them by name. But, like Broker, they would crawl out of the plush woodwork somewhere and contact me if I wanted them to.

Some of what I did for Broker was undoubtedly Mob-related, but only some of it. To the best of my knowledge Broker was not in the direct employ of the Family (or Outfit or Mafia or whatever) and did only piecework for them, assignments that were in some way inconvenient for handling through conventional Family channels. Only rarely would a hit of mine in one of the larger cities, like Chicago or Milwaukee, be Mob-related, as the Family had enough help on the local payroll to handle practically anything; with the smaller-scale Family operations, in cities of less than half a million, outside help through the Broker or someone like him might be called upon. Other than that, the person who came to Broker was your run-of-the-mill, everyday average citizen who has three to seven thousand dollars handy to pay for killing someone he doesn't like.

I had built up no particular philosophy about my work, but then I had no particular problem living with myself, so I didn't really need one. I guess I did develop my own little handful of rationalizations to fall back on, should I need them some rainy day. One of them was that any person somebody wanted dead more than likely deserved it. But I knew that wasn't necessarily true. A better rationalization was that this was just an extension of being a soldier and what I was doing was neither moral nor immoral, but amoral, like war.

Which is a good rationalization, but then you have to rationalize war.

What I realized at the outset as well as later was that certain people are going to want certain other people dead, and what are you going to do? Once somebody decides another somebody is going to have to die, that's the ballgame. All that's left are details.

Anybody I ever hit was set to go anyway. I saw to it that it happened fast and clean. It was something like working in a butcher shop, only my job pays better, the hours are shorter and there isn't the mess.

5

Eddie Robinson said, "Mother of Mercy, is this the end of Rico?" and somebody made a noise outside the motel room, out on the balcony. I eased the volume down on the television and listened: nothing for a moment, then whoever it was knocked at the sliding glass door.

I turned off the set and checked my watch. I'd been looking at the late late show, which was just getting over anyway, and it was ten before two A.M. About right for Broker, though maybe a shade early; I'd expected him to show more like three-thirty or four, when it'd be extremely unlikely anybody'd be up and about to see him come calling.

The knocking continued, got insistent. I swigged down the last of the Coke and got up off the bed, set the empty on the dresser next to the three bottles I'd drained watching the old gangster picture, which wasn't bad at all considering its age. That Robinson guy was a pro, you really had to respect him. But every fifteen minutes two clowns came on and pitched used cars for half an hour, and each time they came on I went out for a Coke. On my way to the door I opened my suitcase on the stand and got out the automatic and held it behind me.

I'd cleaned the gun and switched barrels on it since the afternoon; the silencer was on and clean, too.

I slid the door open a crack and the son of a bitch stuck his foot in and with it slid the glass panel hard open and came in fist-first, and it was a goddamn big fist, the mother of all fists, half-filling my face as it struck. My feet went out from under me and the automatic jumped out of my hand and tumbled under the bed—but the guy hadn't even seen the gun. By the time he was in the door and getting his first look at me, I was on my ass.

My nose was bleeding, not broken but bleeding, and I was stunned. But I could see that the guy's hands were empty, so I didn't dive for the automatic under the bed. I wanted first to play the situation out, at least a few moments' worth.

He was pretty big. Six-two, I'd say, which put him four inches over my head, and he was a solid two hundred pounds in a nicely cut tan business suit. He was around forty or forty-five, with a college fraternity face set under iron-gray short-cropped hair that just missed being a butch. There were no lines on that face, not a one, except where his brow was crinkling over close-set gray eyes that peered out from behind—Christ, yes—dark-framed glasses. What the hell kind of material was Broker sending out, these days?

I tried to wipe the blood away from my nose with my forearm, but more flowed down to take its place, and the stuff was all over my suit. I was a mess. What was the fucking deal? Sure, I gave Broker a bad time, but this sending out strong-arms to hassle me was boondock thinking. I didn't get it, I just didn't. Broker and me understood each other, didn't we? He knew that hard time I gave him back at the restaurant was to let him know I wouldn't be pushed, didn't he?

Then I realized I'd been on the floor five or ten seconds and the guy with glasses hadn't done a damn thing. He was just standing there, brow crinkled, teeth bared, crouching like Tarzan or somebody waiting for his opponent to get up and fight like a man. Good God, was *that* what he was waiting for? Well, fuck him. He could come to me.

I'm no wrestler; I'm no boxer. I weigh a hundred fifty-five and I'm in good shape but nothing spectacular. I've never liked hand-to-hand combat, and I've never mastered any of its subtleties, and I don't have a belt of any color in karate or anything else. But I have an advantage over a lot of guys bigger and stronger than me, when it comes down to a fight, and that's my total lack of principles. When he came over to me thinking the fight was over before it started, I kicked his balls up inside him.

He started in rolling around on the floor, hands between his legs. I pulled his coat down around his shoulders and knocked him cold on the first try. I gave him a fast, thorough frisk. He was unarmed. His billfold had driver's license, credit cards and other identification, all in the name George Swanson, supposedly from St. Paul, Minnesota.

What shit was this?

The phone rang while I was trying to figure it out I picked up the receiver and a voice said, "George?" and I recognized the voice and figured it out and started to laugh.

When I got through laughing, I set the receiver down on the nightstand, the voice squeaking, "George? George!" and hauled George Swanson out into the deserted hall, dumping him down a good ways from my door. Then I went back to the room and picked up the receiver and said, "After what I did to your husband, I don't think he'll be of much use to you for a day or two."

I heard her take air in through her teeth, an angry hissing, a pissed-off snake. In my mind's eye I could see Helen Swanson, and her thin dark naked body, as she said, "Bastard. Jesus Christ prick bastard."

"Now, now."

"You…you…" She sputtered on like that for a while, and there was a strange tone to her voice. Confusion? Fear? Arousal?

"What'd I do, piss you off this afternoon somehow?" I asked the phone. "Or do you do this to all of us? Sit out in your black bikini and sucker us in and then later tell old George about it, so he can play defender of womanhood."

"I only tell him sometimes." Now there was a smile in her voice. It was soft. She was trying to be sexy. "I just tell him when somebody I like doesn't appreciate me."

"Hell, lady, I appreciate you. I really do. You're something else."

"I hope he didn't hurt you."

"No. Not at all. I enjoy getting punched in the nose."

"I...I just told him you made a pass...I didn't know he'd get rough."

"You knew he'd get rough," I said. "That's what he always does, isn't it? Tell me, what's he like when he comes back fresh from beating the hell out of one of your ex-sweeties?"

"He's beautiful," she said. I could almost see the big fat self-indulgent grin she'd have going. "He's mean and he's beautiful. It's the only time I can stand him in bed."

"Well don't expect much from him tonight." Somebody was making noise in the background.

"Someone's at the door," she whispered, in a quick-into-the-closet sort of voice.

"I wonder who it could be," I said.

"Listen..." She laughed softly. "I'm naked right now. What do you think of that?"

"I think it figures."

"After he...falls back asleep, I'll...come up to your room...okay? You owe me that much."

"You come upstairs I got a Coke bottle for you and that's all." I shook my head. "Let him in, will you? He's probably out there bleeding all over the hall. He could use some help."

I hung up.

I retrieved my automatic, switched on the TV again and found nothing going on any of the stations, flicked the set off and stretched out on the bed to wait for the

Broker. Hell, I shouldn't have underestimated Broker like that. Things weren't rough enough yet that he'd stoop to hiring a George Swanson.

I laughed again, but only for a moment. It wasn't really funny, not at all. Disgusting was more like it, the goddamn bitch. But who was I to judge? Takes all kinds to make a world.

6

At four-fifteen Broker came in by the hall entrance. He had company. Without a word he and his friend found chairs and sat and faced me. I closed the door and locked and night-latched it and went to the bed and sat where they would have to turn their chairs to look at me. They did.

"Hello, Quarry," Broker said.

"Broker."

"This is Carl."

This was Carl: a young kid, twenty or twenty-two, with short black serviceman hair just starting to grow out, his complexion powder-white excepting a splotch-circle of red on either cheek which gave him the look of a clown in minimal makeup and was either natural rosiness or the boy was flushed. He was about the size of George Swanson, but leaner and harder-muscled, or at least so I guessed. His jaw was firm, eyes blue-gray. He was wearing a wine-color double-knit sports jacket and gray slacks with a light yellow shirt and a deep yellow tie; I looked at Broker in his gray double-knit suit and light pink shirt and deep pink tie and made a wild guess about who picked out Carl's clothes. The sports jacket did not bulge from the gun under Carl's left arm and I made a mental note to ask Broker sometime who was his tailor.

Carl stood and said, "How are you doing, Quarry?"

There were two things wrong with Carl: one of them was the smell of youthful anxiety that clung to him like dime-store perfume.

I pointed to his left leg, said, "Vietnam?"

He looked flustered, wondering how the hell I knew it was artificial, then nodded. "Hand grenade, I was walking point."

"I asked where, not how."

Broker was one fine American, finding jobs for us boys back from overseas like he did, and now here he was breaking in a handicapped veteran. The man deserved a commendation from the VA or the President or some damn body.

Broker said, "You're still in that foul mood, aren't you?"

I said, "Give me a second and I'll get out the party hats."

Carl sat back down and his cheeks weren't red anymore. That was an improvement.

"What is he supposed to be?" I said.

"He's here with me."

"Oh. Well that explains it."

"Now look…how am I supposed to know what you're up to? You've never acted so damned irrationally, not in many years of what I always considered a good working relationship. But you're acting like a wild man, holding out materials which you've been paid to deliver. Do you have any concept of the value of what you're keeping from me? At any rate, I thought it best to have a man along."

"Why didn't you bring one, then? But no, you drag in

a twelve-year-old gimp, who's supposed to, what? Snap me in line? Beat me to death with his wooden leg?" I checked Carl out of the corner of my eye to see if he reacted; he didn't, which was a sign of hope for the boy.

"Quarry, Quarry…let's not fence." The Broker smiled and the smile was a crease in his face. "Please, I'm tired of fencing with you. After what we've been through together, all of this bickering seems so childish."

"Broker, will you quit acting like this is some goddamn company and I'm going to get a gold watch and a pension after twenty-five years? Have you worked the front office of the fertilizer plant for so long you don't remember it's shit you're selling?"

"You've been paid, Quarry. Don't play with me."

"If you come alone, I wouldn't play. But you're the one playing, Broker. And you keep playing with me and I keep telling you I won't be played with."

Broker looked at Carl and pointed at the door. "Wait outside, Carl."

Carl made a face.

"Go on Carl," he said. "Just out in the hall there will be fine."

Carl got up. He walked to the door. He was pretty good on the leg. Whoever gave him therapy knew what they were doing. I said, "Watch yourself going down steps, kid," and he was out the door, which he nearly—almost, but not quite—slammed.

"You're a damned sadist," Broker said.

"I'm no such thing," I said.

"Riding a kid with one leg, my sweet God."

"You're the sadist," I said, "hiring a kid with one leg. What's the idea? Don't forget, hire the vet?"

"You saw him on it, he's doing an outstanding job. He's better on that artificial limb than most men are with what nature gave them. And he's in tip-top shape otherwise, and he's hard-nosed and handy with firearms. He'll be a good man."

"Doing what? What I do?"

"I don't know yet. I'm grooming him. He's one of the men I keep on the payroll here in town. He's one of two men presently guarding my home, and giving me personal protection."

"Well he may make a bodyguard," I said, "but don't send him out in the field. Not if you want him to last a month, anyway."

"Oh? Really?"

"Oh really. He may be hard-nosed, but he's thin-skinned. You saw his hackles rise when I needled him, didn't you?"

Broker shrugged. "Perhaps you have a point. I don't know, I'll watch him. But I still think he has promise."

"You really think you're doing the kid a favor," I said, "giving him a job."

"You don't seem to think there's anything wrong with this business."

"There isn't, not for me. I didn't get into the trade because I lost a leg, either."

"You lost a wife. Is that so different?"

"Yes. You can grow a new wife."

"You haven't."

I didn't say anything. It was time for getting things out of the way. I dug into my pocket and tossed him an envelope. The key to the locker was in it. Of course the key to the other locker was elsewhere, tucked safely away for my own later use.

"What's this?" Broker said.

I told him what it was, and what was in the locker the key opened.

"Christ almighty, you mean to tell me you left the stuff right there in the airport?"

"Right there. In the airport."

Broker got angry for a moment, said, "What if the police searched the lockers for some reason? After the body was discovered, for example, or in the case of a bomb threat."

"Why, you thinking of calling one in?"

Broker wanted to stay mad, but saw it wouldn't do any good. "I don't know about you, Quarry," he said, like a father disappointed with junior's grades.

I said, "You going to send Carl after the stuff? You and I can wait here."

"I'll have to go myself."

"Yourself? You're full of balls in your old age, Broker, what's got into you?"

"I can trust myself."

"And you can't trust Carl? Broker, I'm ashamed of you. Talking that way about a disabled veteran."

"Go to hell, Quarry. I'm sending Carl up to keep you company. Any objections?"

Why bother? "No," I said.

So Broker went out and Carl came in. He got settled back in his chair and sat there and gave me a hard look, which he'd no doubt been practicing outside while he thought about me and the remarks I'd made about him and his leg, or lack of same.

Finally he let it out. He said, "What the hell you got against one-legged guys, anyway?"

"Four of them got together and gangbanged my sister."

"Aw eat shit, Quarry, can't you answer straight just once?"

"I got nothing against one-legged guys," I said. "It's just you I can't stand."

"Oh, oh, really? And, and what's wrong with me?"

"Don't ask me for reasons. Don't ever ask me for reasons."

"I don't think I ever met any bigger bastard than you, Quarry. You're one big fucking bastard."

"Army teach you to talk that way? Really foul stuff like that? Shocking."

"You just shut up."

"What?"

"You shut up, I said."

"Didn't Broker tell you what I am?"

"He told me."

"Then you ought to know better than to tell me to shut up."

"I'll tell you again."

"You tell me again and I'll come over there and feed you that wooden leg."

His eyes got big. "It's…not wooden. It's not a wooden leg."

"What the hell would you call it?"

"A prosthesis."

"Whatever."

"What…what the hell makes you hate me?"

"I didn't say I hated you."

"Oh? What then?"

"I said I couldn't stand you."

"There's a difference?"

"Yeah."

"Such as?"

"Such as I don't waste energy hating you. But I can't stand to look at you, because you're an asshole, and I don't like looking at assholes…now that's all the explanation you're going to get, so leave it alone."

He did. He got quiet and folded his hands in his lap and sat there thinking, trying to understand what it was he did that made me want to give him so bad a time. I didn't know why myself. I just knew this kid was going to die and somewhere in the back of my head, somewhere it seemed vaguely a waste.

But die he would. Like anybody who goes into it for any other reason than to make money. There's no room for revenge. No leeway for crusades. You can't kill people because you hated your daddy or because you saw mammy screwing the milkman when you were five or because when you were six a bully took your wagon away from you or because you want back the leg some other mindless idiot blew off for some mindless idiotic nonreason. You last only if you don't care. If you care, if you have to care about something, care about money. Money and your ass.

7

Dawn was poking at the sky. I was standing at the glass door to the balcony, drawing back the curtain and watching the colors of the sky change and reflect and shimmer on the water of the pool below. I hoped I'd be able to get in another swim before I left.

An hour or so had passed and Carl and I had stopped trying to make conversation. It got to the point where either we'd have to get friendly or keep quiet, and I wasn't about to get friendly. The air was so heavy with mutual hostility I was almost relieved when the single, soft knock came at the hall entrance. I went to the dresser and got open the drawer where I'd stashed the nine-millimeter automatic and took it out and Carl's eyes flickered. I walked to the door, the gun behind me.

Broker came in and with one quick motion dismissed Carl, who was only too glad to go. I put the automatic away and sat on the bed. Broker selected a chair and brought it up close to where I sat. He took off his suitcoat and folded it across his lap, folded his hands. He looked at me. He looked at me hard, his eyes moving toward the center of his face, all but crossing.

"Well, Quarry?"

"Well, Broker."

"That was all."

"You asking or telling or what?"

"The one bag. Was that all?"

"Of course it was all."

"There should have been more."

"Is that right?"

"That's right."

"How much more should there have been, Broker?"

"Another bag."

"Oh?"

"Another bag of the same size."

"There was only the one."

"Are you sure?"

"Yes."

"Positive?"

"How many times do I have to answer the same question, Broker?"

"Until I believe you, Quarry."

"There was one bag. One bag, Broker. I won't fool with that stuff, you know that, don't you?"

"I thought I did. Where did he keep it?"

"Well, I had to search him. He claimed he shipped the stuff out by some other route. Said he didn't have any of it on him. But I shook him down and found that bag in the lining of his coat."

"Some other route. Did he say what route?"

"No. When he said that, I didn't pursue it. I thought he was bullshitting. And when I found the bag on him, I was convinced."

"Do you remember what it was he said?"

"No."

"What did he say, exactly?"

"I don't remember, exactly."

"Quarry…are you being straight with me? Can I trust you you're telling the truth?"

"You'll have to."

"If you're lying, I can get it out of you."

"If I'm lying, you can't, Carl can't, and nobody you know can."

He thought that over. A tic got going, gently, under his left eye; he touched his mustache. He decided what I said was true; he decided Quarry was so tough no man alive could make him talk. Wrong. There are guys so fucking mean they could look at me and I'd tell them whatever they wanted to know. But Broker didn't know that, so it didn't matter.

"Broker," I said, "I've been working through you for, what, now? Five years? Have I ever tried to pull one single damn thing on you?"

Broker shook his head no.

"And," I said, "haven't I told you I didn't want to be involved in any part of anything except this one thing I do? Just my one thing. We've talked about that several times. Few hours ago, at that restaurant, for instance."

Broker nodded.

"So what do you think?" I said.

Broker hesitated. Then he touched his hands to his knees and said, "I think we ought to forget this matter."

"Good."

"I think we ought to forget this matter and get on to something else."

"Good."

Broker seemed to relax; the tic was gone; he touched his mustache again, but in a different way. He said, "This afternoon, at the airport, was a rather hastily conceived affair. You were, of course, called in for another purpose entirely. But with you available, I felt it less than prudent to use someone local, like Carl, who wouldn't have been able to perform in the professional manner I can depend upon you to employ."

"Thanks for the orchids," I said. "Now what about the assignment you had in mind before the sidetrack?"

Broker nodded and said, "Your associate is already doing preliminary work."

"Boyd's there already?"

"Yes. Mr. Boyd has been on the scene for a week. You can join him tomorrow afternoon…" Broker glanced at his watch. "Rather, I should say, this afternoon."

"He's not somewhere here in the Cities, is he?"

"No. One hit this close to home…my home, that is…is dangerous enough, let alone two. But you will be closer than perhaps is best. Thirty miles from here, small town of twenty or twenty-two thousand, on the Iowa side."

"Port City?" I asked.

"Yes. You know it?"

"Been through it. Wouldn't say I know it. Just another river town, little smaller, little older than some I worked."

"A very simple assignment, really. You'll need three, four days at most."

"Fine."

Broker unfolded his suitcoat and got an envelope out from a side pocket and handed it to me. "There's a piece of paper in there, with a phone number on it."

I took the envelope and folded it and stuck it in my shirt pocket. "Boyd's number?"

Broker nodded.

"Motel or hotel or what?"

"Phone rings where he's doing surveillance. He'll be there most of the time."

"A phone at a lookout? Sounds like an unusual situation."

"It is. It's a dream situation for you, Quarry, like a vacation with pay."

"Work isn't my idea of a vacation, and neither is Port City."

"Busman's holiday, then." Broker got up and into his suitcoat, smoothing it with his palms and saying, "Sorry we had so much trouble with that other matter."

"All is forgiven, Broker."

"I'm sorry if you found your task today offensive. I'll keep that in mind and avoid giving you any such activities in the future."

"Good."

"Enjoy your stay in Port City."

"I don't enjoy my work, Broker. I just do it."

Broker smiled. "And you do it well, Quarry. I appreciate

that. You didn't even bother asking how much this one's going to pay."

"Doesn't matter. I'm sure you've told Boyd all that. It'll give us something to talk about."

Broker walked to the door. "Quarry."

"Yes?"

"Let me ask you something."

"Go ahead."

"Why does it bother you so much, my hiring Carl?"

"Doesn't bother me at all," I said.

He shook his head, shrugged and opened the door, where Carl was outside waiting. The kid glanced at me and I gave him the peace sign and shut the door on them.

8

I left the Quad Cities at three-thirty that afternoon. I drove down the Illinois side, along a moderately traveled road bordered by lush farmland, busy with harvesters; an occasional cluster of trees bent over green and graceful in the less than gentle afternoon breeze, like oversize, out-of-shape ballet dancers trying in vain to touch distant toes.

I crossed the suspension bridge over the Mississippi River—though it was more suspense than suspension, as it was a rickety, narrow, mostly wooden old thing that had to date back to horse-and-buggy days—and found myself in the heart of Port City's business district. I set aside an hour and started driving, aimlessly guiding my gray rental Ford over and around Port City; when the hour was up I felt for a stranger I knew the little town pretty good, and why not? It was the same as a thousand other small towns. Not unlike the one I grew up in.

Port City was two hills with a downtown in between, with growths extending from each corner of the city, one to the north a prosperous shopping-center boomtown, one to the south a slum-ridden embarrassment to the Chamber of Commerce. The latter section of the city was in fact called South End, and only by small-town

Midwestern standards could it be classified a slum; in big cities used to ghettos and such, South End would've been a residential neighborhood. From a Port City point of view, it was a clapboard eyesore, saved only by the beginnings of commercial growth at the town's southern-most tip.

East Hill ran mostly to aging but still distinguished-looking brick and/or wooden two-stories, and was very much middle class, while West Hill had apparently once been the home of the elite, and no doubt still was to some extent; while the young rich might choose to move into one of the classier of the housing additions dotting the northwest edge of town, the older guard would probably be content to remain in the elegant near-mansions of West Hill, old nineteenth-century beauties full of char-acter, many of the best ones overlooking the bend of the river Port City was situated along.

The downtown, in the valley of the two hills, bordered on either side by factories, was more death rattle than business district; ancient buildings wore shiny new front-of-the-store bottom-floor facades, like terribly old men boasting terribly new false teeth. This collective face-lift was undoubtedly inspired by the shopping mall on the north end of town, where East Hill exploded into fran-chise restaurants and gas stations and motels and auto dealerships.

There was a building downtown, on a corner across from two churches and the post office, that looked like a prefab grammar school got out of hand. It was the YMCA.

Next to the sterile, dull Y, extending down to the other
corner, was a huge gothic brick-and-stone building with a
long stone stairway that in three tiers led up to archway
doors: the city library. It was being torn down. A guy
inside the cab of a metal monster was smacking a big
black steel ball into the building's side, and there was a
crunching groan of a sound each time the ball hit. Some
people were standing around watching, leaning up against
a fence that squared in the work area; a billboard just
back of the fence, over to the left, showed a drawing of
the projected new library, which looked to be a twin of its
YMCA neighbor, but bigger and pointlessly angular, some
computer's idea of design. Most of the people had neu-
tral looks on their faces, others looked vaguely pissed off.
One longhaired kid flipped the bird to the guy working
the ball. Stupid. If you want to finger somebody, I thought,
finger the asshole who ordered the place torn down; say
fuck you to the asshole who shoved a new library down
the town's throat, the city manager whose brother-in-law
runs a cement factory, or the empire-building librarian
who'll get a better job somewhere else because he got
Port City a new library, or the alderman whose firm did
the electrical work, or whatever bureaucratic bastards
cause the trouble here. Not the guy working the ball.

I parked in front of the Y and went in. The outside of
the building was light-brown brick and the reception
area was more of the same, but with blue metal trim and
white ceiling tile trimmed with black metal. The atmosphere was homey, like a reformatory remodeled by a

contractor who wanted more money than he was getting. I knew the pool must be close by because the air was full of chlorine and little kids with suits wrapped in towels were scooting around bumping into things and each other. A three-walled fortress of a desk enclosed and protected an office, which had a windowless door, shut. Standing behind the desk, leaning on the counter reading *Zap Comix,* was a skinny, younger-than-middle-aged guy with white shoulder-length hair and matching bushy beard, though the mustache was black and so were the eyebrows and streaks of black were elsewhere in his hair. He was wearing a long-sleeve lumberjack plaid shirt, and both shirt and beard seemed out of place in summer, but then maybe he stayed in where it was air-conditioned most of the time. Now I knew what Gabby Hayes must have looked like as a young man, something I hadn't been dying to find out.

I said, "I'm going to be in town for a few days. Do you have a room for me?"

The bushy head wagged affirmative. By looking real close at the young old man I could see he was enjoying the comic: his eyes had crinkles at the corners and the mustache was turning up at the ends.

"Can I use the pool while I stay here?"

"You mean for swimming?" he said, finally looking up at me but still not really listening.

"No," I said. "In case I wake up thirsty in the middle of the night."

"Sure, man, you can use the pool." He looked back

down at the comic, then continued: "Course you'll have to work yourself around our schedule. Afternoon swim classes and Saturday morning swim classes, and Businessman's Swim Wednesday night, and Thursday night Family Night."

I wondered what threat I might pose to Family Night, but let it pass. "How much in advance?"

"One day's worth. Four."

I gave him five and he gave me change. He had me sign a name in a book and he got a key for me from a board which was stuck up against the wall next to the office door. "Room's upstairs," he said, and he pointed, looking back down at the *Zap.* I followed his finger to the stairway at the end of the hall.

Up on the dorm floor, I found a pay phone next to a Coke machine. I used both. Sipping at the can of Coke, I dialed the number Broker had given me.

"…yes?"

The hesitant voice was Boyd's.

"I'm in town."

"Hey, Quarry. Good enough."

"How's it going?"

"Smooth. Remember St. Louis?"

"Yeah."

"That smooth. Smoother than that."

"Where are you?"

"You know this town at all?"

"I drove around a while."

"Remember seeing a dump called Binelli's?"

"A cigar store?"

"Yeah, with a bar in it."

"Taco joint across the street?"

"That's the one. It's the building next to Binelli's. An old chiro's got an office on the bottom floor. I'm up on the third."

"Front or back entrance?"

"There's a front way in, but come around the alley way. There's a wooden stairway comes right up to the back door."

"You need me immediately or anything?"

"Not really."

"Let me get settled then. Maybe catch an hour or two of sleep. Look for me round seven, okay?"

"Okay. Hey, Quarry?"

"What."

"You like tacos?"

"Not especially."

"Pick some up before you come up."

"Oh Christ."

"Ah come on, I been smelling that taco smell till I could go crazy. Come on and pick up a couple orders, goddamnit. I'm sick of eating my own cooking."

"You got a place to *cook* there?"

"Sure. I'm staying right here, too. There's room for you, Quarry. I suppose you're staying at the Y, Jesus."

"What're you doing, sleeping on the floor?"

"You know me better than that. There's twin beds here."

"Twin beds? And you're cooking? What the hell kind of lookout is that?"

"Come see."

"Okay. Seven."

"Seven. Tacos, Quarry?"

"We'll see."

I hung up and finished off the can of Coke and dumped it in a trash can. Then I went down to my room, which was small and clean and new but about the size of a closet; the floor was scuff-marked tile, and the furniture—what there was of it—was that kind of wood that looks like plastic. I unpacked, put my stuff in the dresser, except for the nine-millimeter, which with a few other odds and ends I left locked in my briefcase and shoved under the bed. I set my little travel alarm for an hour and got settled down for a nap. When the alarm went off, I'd go down and see if the pool was free. After my swim I'd join Boyd.

9

Boyd was homosexual. I figured I better tell you right off, rather than sneak up on it. Queer as a three-dollar bill, but he never tried anything with me, so I didn't give a damn. His life was his.

I couldn't help but wonder whether or not Broker knew about Boyd's sex leaning when he teamed him up with me. Later, when I told Broker about Boyd, he acted surprised and asked me did I want somebody different to work with and I said no thanks, Boyd's different enough as it is. After I gave it some further thought, I realized Broker had to be playing dumb—which was typical of him—since his research into each man he took on was nothing short of phenomenal. Somehow he figured I wouldn't mind Boyd, whereas somebody else would. He was right. Boyd could sleep with sheep if he had a mind to, so long as he didn't fuck me or the job.

From the first I had suspicions about that side of him, and they must've showed, because before long Boyd came right out and told me. But he said not to worry, though, said he was "married" and didn't do any playing around. Out of bits and pieces of what he said over the years, I came to know that his "wife" was a gay hairdresser he lived with somewhere back east.

Boyd was a pro, and his sex life he didn't let interfere

with business. Sure, I had thoughts about the sexual implications of his being in this line of work; the idea of a bullet entering a man's body being a kind of symbol for penetration, sexually speaking I mean. Which is Freudian bullshit. For one thing, Boyd was as cold as I was about the actual carrying out of an assignment; he took no pleasure from his work, or at least revealed no overt signs of emotion. For another thing, he preferred back-up position, which generally entailed no actual violence whatsoever. The back-up does the watching, gets the mark's schedule down pat and then covers while somebody like me does the actual job. Every fourth assignment, Boyd would take the active role as hitman and I'd take over in the passive back-up position, so he could keep his hand in, should our team get split and he have to go with another partner.

The funny thing is you'd never know from looking at him he was that way. You couldn't tell from his personality, either, unless you paid real close attention. He was a little guy, five-six or so, but broad-shouldered and solid-built, his features on the rough side, including a nose that had been broken a couple times in this barroom brawl and that one, and a flat, scarred face that looked to have seen its share of problems. His hair was thick and brown and curly, and his mustache and eyebrows were bushy, his eyes a gunmetal black with a hard cast to them. His eyelashes were the only remotely feminine thing about him, being long and heavy, but they seemed to add to an overall darkly handsome, rugged-hewn quality that made broads want to climb in his pants.

Which is one of the ways I got tipped to realizing he was that way. Several times we were in bars and good-looking chicks'd snuggle up to him—not hard-faced hookers, either, but nice stuff. He'd act cold. Not just cold, but repulsed. And this was back when Broker first got the two of us together, so we could talk and get to know each other and discuss how we'd handle the team-up, should we agree to it. So these were almost social occasions, when he was turning his nose up at this playmate material. Had he acted that way later on, on the job, I'd have thought nothing of it; some guys could very naturally want to stay away from sex on a job. I'm not one of them, but I can understand it. Boxers have been known to make like priests for a month or two before a big fight. Personally I find a piece of ass, while I'm waiting in some town to do my number, helps drain off some of the tension that builds up in me, below the surface.

Boyd and I got along well. He was easy to get along with, very undemanding. Really was kind of a bland guy, ordinary in every way. The kind of guy who follows his favorite team and gets upset when they lose a game. The kind of guy who always asks for Budweiser. The kind of guy who wears a lumpy brown suit from off the rack and then tries to jazz it up a little with a colorful tie, in last year's width.

But I respected him because he did his job well. He felt the same about me. He was a very good lookout, because he seemed to have a natural streak of Peeping Tom in him that I just don't have. I get bored in the back-up position. Stakeout shit puts me to sleep, and consequently I tend to miss things, which is dangerous. And Boyd could tail a man, even in a small town like Port City, without having his presence felt one iota. I guess it's his size, since his looks would seem distinctive enough to attract attention. Of course I'm not particularly big, either, but then tailing somebody is a job for a sneak, which I'm not, and a patient man, which I'm also not. Boyd was not only patient, but a born sneak. It was a pleasure working with him.

However.

On our last job, a couple months back, he'd been way below par. I had a hunch his "marriage" was on the rocks, from little between-the-lines things I could read in what he said. He drank while on lookout, for one thing. He didn't get plastered or anything, but even sipping along a beer, especially beer after beer, can dull your senses. And your senses got to be keen when you're working back-up, for Christ's sake.

I didn't like it. I wasn't afraid he was going to make a pass at me or something—it wasn't that. I was afraid he was going to make a mistake. Some half-ass mistake that would kill us both.

When I came up to my room after my swim and got dressed, I was thinking about Boyd, and how he'd been acting. He sounded normal enough on the phone, but that half-ass edge was in his voice. Somehow I knew this would have to be my last job with Boyd.

But first I'd have to get this job—whatever the hell it was—out of the way. And right now I had to go out and pick up some fucking tacos.

10

I climbed the wooden steps and stopped on the second-floor landing to glance inside: nothing, the apartment below Boyd was vacant. That was good. I went on up to the next landing and tried Boyd's door. Unlocked. That was not so good. I locked the door behind me and walked easily, quietly through the dark apartment, which was three large rooms laid out in a row, like a boxcar: kitchen, bedroom, living room. The place was furnished modestly but well, with a distinctly feminine flair in the colors and even the faintly perfumy smell everything had, especially the bedroom. The walls were pink stucco and the floors were carpeted. A nice, well-above-average apartment, that looked lived in.

I found Boyd in the living room sitting to the side of double windows that looked out onto the street. The neons and such out there kept the room semilit. He was leaned against the wall, the trunk of his body twisted so it faced me, his head turned so he could peer from out the corner of the window; if I sat that way I'd get a crick in my neck that would take that chiro downstairs a month to rid me of, but Boyd always sat that way when he was watching, one pillow between his back and the wall, another snuggled under his butt. At his feet was a paperback folded open, cover-side up, next to a can of beer; the paperback was called *Twilight Love* and the beer was Budweiser. He was wearing floppy brown slacks and a yellow short-sleeve shirt with a green tie and he needed a haircut. I tossed the sack of tacos at him.

He jumped. He couldn't have jumped higher if I goosed him. Which was something I wasn't about to do, considering how he was liable to take it. "Shit! Shit!" he said. "Quarry."

"You dumb asshole," I said. "What in hell was that back door doing unlocked?"

His face got squinched up, but before irritation could climb out of him, his nose got scent of the tacos and he smiled. He reached down and picked up the bag and opened it and peeked in and said, "Hey, Quarry, you're all right. You brought the tacos. Hey."

"Hey. I brought the tacos. Now what about the damn door?"

He made a farting sound with his lips. "Who else is going to show but you, Quarry? I just unlocked the door about five minutes ago. No sweat."

"I'm worried about you, Boyd."

"Aw, can it."

"Aren't you supposed to be watching out that window?"

"Hey, who appointed you foreman all of the goddamn sudden?"

"Don't push me, Boyd."

The irritation came back and got out: "Bullshit! I been cooped up watching a whole goddamn week, you break *your* ass watching for a while."

"So that's your trick: you watch with your ass."

"Oh fuck you. I'm going out to the kitchen and eat my tacos."

"Do that."

"I will."

"But before you do, maybe you might tell me who I'm supposed to be watching."

"Oh. Sure. Little ginky guy, about five-eight."

"Three inches taller than you, you mean."

"God, you're a fucker."

"Never mind that. Tell me some more about him."

"What more? That's it, just a gink, and a blind gink at that, always wears tinted glasses. Usually wears gray slacks and a cardigan sweater."

"A cardigan sweater? In the summer?"

"Yeah. It's got those diamond-shape type of patterns on it, in shades of gray. Damn thing looks like a big argyle sock." Boyd snickered.

"Shit, it's eighty degrees out there."

"Naw, it's cool tonight, but this guy leaves the sweater on even when it's hot. It was up to ninety two days ago and he still had the sweater on."

"Sounds like an oddball."

"Believe me, we're doing the world a favor on this one."

"Is it his apartment you're watching, or what?"

"Yeah. The building right across from us, but down a floor. There's a do-it-yourself laundry below him and another apartment, empty, above him."

I went over to the window, standing to the side

against the wall. I looked out. This was a weird commercial district, kind of off to one side of the downtown, on one of the streets running perpendicular to the river and just on the border of a dip where factories and plants took over down to the edge of the slope of East Hill. On the corner, to the right, was a fancy drugstore, taking up a quarter of the block, its tall display windows full of expensive gift-shop-type items. Next to it was an incongruously sleazy bar, and then the VFW hall, and another bar, and the taco joint, and the laundry, and a coin wash.

I said, "The second floor, there? Where the light is on and kind of yellowish?"

"Yeah. His eyes are bad, wears tinted glasses remember, and near as I can tell all the light bulbs in his apartment are yellow like that."

"You feel you got his pattern down pretty good?"

Boyd nodded, confident. "He won't be coming out again tonight, until quarter to nine. Then he walks down to that drugstore and has a soda at their fountain. Or at least that's what he had the two times I followed him in and watched him up close."

"A soda."

"Yeah. Thank God I got a refrigerator full of beer here, or I'd go nuts walking by a bar to go into a drugstore for a soda." Thinking of it, Boyd came over and leaned down and got his can of Bud, then, as an afterthought, picked up his paperback as well. He said, "You go ahead and watch a while. Yell if he starts to leave or something."

I sat down. No need to play contortionist like Boyd: it

would be easy watching from here, since this window on the third floor was well above street eye-level, and safely above second-floor level.

"Quarry?"

"Are you still in here?"

"It's…good to see you."

"Is it."

"You're pissed off, aren't you?"

"No."

"What're you pissed off about?"

"Nothing."

"You think I let you down last time, don't you?"

"You didn't let me down."

"You think I did. You think I didn't watch that guy in Toledo as close as I could've. You think if I'd done my part you wouldn't almost've got seen leaving when those people showed at the place next door."

"We been all over that."

"Have we?"

"We have."

"I'm telling you, Quarry, you can watch a mark for a week, two weeks, and you can get his life down fairly well, but there's always going to be a joker or two turn up in the deck, you know? Hell you could watch a year and stuff could *still* crop up. The unexpected, right? You got to expect it."

"Your tacos are getting cold."

"Okay. How much do I owe you?"

"For what?"

"The tacos."

"Christ!"

"Okay, okay." He trudged out of the room.

I turned away as he did and watched. A shadow slowly shuffled across the yellow window across the way. Then nothing. I watched.

11

The yellow window went black.

"Just turned out the lights, didn't he?"

I cocked my head and looked at Boyd. He was glancing at his wristwatch and he had a wiggly little grin going under his curly brown mustache. He was showing off: from where he was, stretched out on the davenport against the wall behind me, sipping his latest Budweiser, he couldn't see the window that had just gone dark. But he wanted me to know what a swell job he was doing, how perfect he knew the mark's pattern. How just checking the time he could tell me what the mark was doing. I could almost feel on my own face the heat from his semi-drunken glow.

"Yeah," I said, turning back around, keeping my back to Boyd, keeping up my vigil.

"You might as well not bother watching anymore."

"Oh?"

"The lights won't be on again. He won't be going out again either. He's got a clock built in him, this gink does. And a boring damn clock it is."

I looked at Boyd. I sat and leaned my shoulders against the wall and folded my arms and said, slowly, "Maybe you been at this too long."

"What the hell's that supposed to mean?"

"It means you're getting sloppy." I glanced back out the window, making a pretense of keeping up my watch on the apartment across the way, just to let Boyd know I didn't trust his judgment anymore.

"Aw bullshit, Quarry. Bullshit. You're the one's been in it too long. You're getting old and paranoid."

"I'm getting old? Christ, you got fifteen fucking years on me, Boyd."

"Age is a state of mind."

"Is it."

"It sure as hell is. Take the mark over there," he said, gesturing toward the window, "he was a hundred years old the day he was born. He's supposed to be thirty-five but he walks around stooped over and shambles along with his head down like he's looking for a hole to curl up and die in. He isn't a man, he's a tombstone walking around."

When he said that it was all I could do to keep from laughing. Because as he spoke he was sprawled out on the davenport, hanging loosely over its edge, like a cadaver somebody was playing a morbid ventriloquist's joke with.

I said, "Maybe it's time you told me something about him."

Boyd nodded, sat up a little. "He's thirty-five or so, like I said. No wife. No friends I seen so far. No social life whatever. Works ungodly hours, about half-time, at a plant in the part of this town they call South End."

"What kind of plant?"

"Something to do with food. He goes there at five in the morning and gets out round ten. He spends the rest of his day walking around the downtown."

"Every day?"

"Yeah. And don't think I've enjoyed getting up at four-thirty A.M. like that gink over there. Shit."

"What does he do in the afternoon, exactly? When he walks around downtown."

"Oh, he's got his little daily routine. He goes to Woolworth's after work for his lunch. It's about eleven when he gets there, and he beats the noon rush that way, and has the waitresses to himself. He likes to pester them, in a gentle kind of way. They laugh at him behind his back but treat him pretty decent to his face. After that he walks from Woolworth's to the Baskin-Robbins ice cream shop out at the Port City Mall."

"The shopping center, you mean?"

"Right."

"Christ, that's some walk."

"Tell me about it. Anyway, he goes there and has a banana split, even though there's a chubby kid behind the counter who cracks up laughing every time he walks in. But he doesn't seem to notice, or mind anyway. When he's through he walks back downtown. By that time it's two-thirty. He goes to a place called Hermann's, which is sort of a drugstore but no prescriptions. But everything else a drugstore has, from Tampax to comic books. And a fountain, where he sits and has a Coke and bothers the

waitresses, who put up with him. He spends an hour
there, so at three-thirty he sets out for the hospital,
where he has a piece of pie at the hospital lunch counter.
He enjoys himself there because the help changes every
day as it's local housewives doing volunteer work for a
hospital auxiliary and so he's treated pretty nice by them,
since they're public-service-minded and don't have to see
him day after day, like the other waitresses he comes up
against. At four-fifteen he starts walking back downtown
and ends up at the *Port City Journal*, where he buys a
paper fresh off the presses from the coin machine out
front. By four-thirty he's back to his apartment where he
goes up to read his paper or jack off or whatever. Anyway,
he comes back out at six-thirty and here's where his day
gets exciting: he chooses, at random, what restaurant he's
going to eat his supper at. At random means one of four
places, but I'll give him credit for breaking pattern here,
as in the week I been on his ass he's jumped around irreg-
ular between the four."

"What about Sunday?"

"Well, I'm only going by one Sunday, mind you, but
I'd guess it's typical for him. He goes to the Methodist
church and sits in a back pew. He wears a gray sportcoat
and brown pants. He goes to the drugstore there on the
corner and has a soda and buys the *Chicago Tribune* and
the *Des Moines Register*. He disappears into his apartment until three, when he walks out to the park to watch
the Little League game at four. When that's over he starts
walking down to the stadium in South End...another

nice walk…where he watches the local semipro team play a game at eight o'clock. For supper he has a hot dog at the stadium stand. And I use the word stadium loosely."

I scratched my head. "He always walks?"

"Unless somebody offers him a ride. Which is rare."

"Maybe he likes to walk."

"Maybe. Anyway he doesn't own a car."

"What do you suppose he does at that plant?"

"Not sure, but it's something in the line of janitorial work or clean-up or something. He's there in between shifts. A group works till five when he shows, and another comes in at ten when he leaves. Since it's food preparation, maybe he cleans the big basins or whatever. I didn't find a way to check the place out too close."

"Is that a big plant he works at?"

"Not particularly. One-story building, kind of medium-size. About twenty on each shift, by the way."

"I don't get this."

"Neither do I."

"Who'd want to kill a nothing like this guy? Why erase a zero?"

"Ours is not to reason why."

That was the first sensible thing Boyd had said lately and almost restored my faith in him. Almost.

I said, "You're right, it's none of our business who hired us and why. Maybe all the waitresses this guy bugs got together and put out a contract on him, who knows? It's not our concern. But…"

"But?"

"But this whole set-up is fucked over. Like this place… what are you doing at a lookout where you're cooking meals and sleeping? What are you doing inside a furnished apartment, obviously lived in, like this one?"

"Who knows? Who cares? All I know is Broker gave me the address and a key to the back door. He didn't give me any explanation, except that it was entirely safe. He said I was to say I was subletting the apartment from…" He thought. "…well I don't remember the name off-hand, but I got it written down somewhere. Carol something, I think it was."

Bad. Christ, Boyd was getting bad.

"Anyway, Broker said the owner of the building, and the broad I'm supposedly subletting it from, would cover for me should anybody official ask. In the meantime, naturally, I'd leave town at once and we'd scratch the hit."

"Does anybody know you're here?"

"Not really."

"What's that supposed to mean?"

"Well Broker knows, and I assume whoever hired us knows."

Standard Operating Procedure was that the identity of our employer not be known to us. There were many reasons for that, most of them obvious, most providing various kinds of protection for the employer. But it also meant that we knew nothing of the motivation behind our action.

Another part of S.O.P. was that Broker—the middleman our employer contacted—received a twenty-five percent down payment, which was his share of the fee; later, at a designated drop point, we would pick up the balance. But only after a lookout had had time to survey the situation and decide whether or not all systems were go. Should Boyd, for example, stake out a mark and decide the job was either impossible or just too damn risky, we would back out and Broker would return all but a minimal fee for his and our time. Once Boyd, or someone like him, gave the go-ahead for the hit, a day would be set and the employer contacted, one way or another, and the rest of the payment made. *Prior* to the actual carrying out of the assignment. Cash up front or no hit. This was my policy, at least. Mine and Boyd's.

"Listen," I said, "is the drop all set for our money?"

"It sure is."

"Where?"

"It'll be in a garbage can right out back of this place, the day we make our move."

"Is the exact day already set?"

"Yes. I called in today."

"Don't you think you should have waited for me? So we could've decided together, like usual?"

"Aw piss, this was so cut-and-dry, Quarry. Come on. Besides, I told Broker if you had other feelings I'd call him back and tell him about change of plans, if any. You and I'll decide that."

"All right," I said. "But somehow I don't like the smell of this thing, or the feel of it or something."

"You're paranoid."

He looked very young right then, the curly head of hair and eyebrows and mustache pasted on, like a kid dressing up like an adult for Halloween.

I said, "Let me tell you something, Boyd."

"What?"

"Something's changed with you. I don't know what it is. Your personal life maybe. I don't know. But unless you get back to normal...by which I mean your normal efficient self...you and I, Boyd, we're getting a divorce."

Boyd sat up. Even in the dark I could see his face had gone white.

"We been together a long time, Quarry."

"I know," I said. "Maybe too long."

12

Bunny's was a bar and restaurant on the outskirts of South End, with a pizza place on one side and a Laundromat on the other, neighbors distant as well as disparate, as between them the three took up land enough for a block and a half of town. The businesses down there on the fringes of Port City were clean and mostly recent-built, and Bunny's was no exception: a handsome dark wood single-story building, perched on a little hilly lawn with an almost absurdly large parking lot surrounding it. Long smoke-color windows fronted the street with not a solitary plastic beer sign in sight, and on both sides of the building, spotlight-lit and painted in big blue block letters, was the word Bunny's.

It was approaching eleven-thirty when I pulled into the lot which had seemed oversize to me when I drove by that afternoon but right now was jampacked. I had no easy time finding a parking place and settled for one a good walk from the door and counted myself lucky. As I neared the building I heard rock music faintly and then the door opened and as some people came out so did the music, loud but not too loud and well-played by a live combo of drum-bass-guitar.

I was relieved to hear rock rather than country western,

and not from my being a supporter or detractor of either cause, but because my experience has been that rock bars run to fewer fights than country western. I don't really know why. It almost seems the more violent the music, the less violent the crowd. And with the rock bar's younger patrons you'll sometimes find a moderate amount of parking-lot pot-smoking going on, which can make for a scattering of sleepy happy people who seem to spread gentle, passive vibrations through a crowd; in a country bar a similar scattering of drunken unhappy people can send a wave of irritation through a crowd that can result in anything from a scuffle to a brawl.

Which was why when I'd driven around town this afternoon, I kept my eyes open for a place like Bunny's. A place where I could sit and drink and get quietly drunk and maybe pick up some broad who didn't have hair sprayed into a style that died in 1961 everywhere else but Iowa.

Wouldn't have done to choose too high-class a bar, either, like the hotel cocktail lounge or something of that sort. Too much chance I could get cornered by some Port City V.I.P. who might get friendly about why-ya-in-town and what-business-ya-in, or worse yet, some Chamber of Commerce smiler full of talk/shit. None of that would do. I wanted to be invisible.

Like my mark was invisible. Like Albert Leroy. That was his name, the mark. Albert Leroy. The man who wore a gray sweater in the summer and got his rocks off watching a Little League ballgame at the park and drinking a soda at the drugstore.

It didn't make sense, it didn't make fucking sense. Invisible people nobody wants to kill. Sometimes—like in my case—you get invisible because you want nobody to notice you. But other guys are born that way. Other guys the doctors yank from the womb and can't see an ass to slap.

This was working on my mind as I walked into Bunny's. This and the way Boyd was acting, the little things out on the edges of the way Boyd was behaving, the little things out on the borders of the job that made no logical sense.

But sometimes there isn't anything you can do about a situation. Except forget about it. And go out and get drunk. Or laid. Or both. And hopefully that was what I'd get done at Bunny's.

Bunny's was two establishments masquerading as one. Two very different dens of iniquity shared a common roof and served two crowds who peacefully coexisted, thanks to having the bar half in the front of the building, where everything was smoky windows and rock music and laughter and noise, and the quiet cocktail lounge-restaurant area in the back half, separated by a little anteroom that housed joint toilet facilities for both worlds and kept the loudness of the bar out of the lounge and included a side entry for those who wished to totally avoid exposure to the rougher element.

But my first impression was of the bar section, which served that younger, wilder set, with the rock band playing against the wall to my left on a postage-stamp platform in front of a postage-stamp dance floor that was full of moving bodies, with chairs and tiny tables and people all bunched close in listening to the combo and swilling down beer. Everyone was dressed casually, almost sloppy in a careless, campus sort of way, blue jeans everywhere you looked, and the only person in the room who didn't fit the college-age, college-look was the blonde.

The blonde was sitting in the corner, with a table to herself next to the stage, her eyes on the drummer of the rock combo. She'd been given more breathing room than anyone else around, perhaps out of respect to her beauty. Turned-up nose, flashing white teeth, long-lashed big blue eyes. Hair white blond and patently unreal but beautiful in a plastic sort of way. Stacked but petite. The best overall one-word description for her was "cute," but she bore her cuteness in an aloof, almost disdainful way. She was smoking and wearing a dark blue pants suit, the top half of which was folded across her lap and a fuzzy baby-blue short-sleeve sweater caressed her bosom; that she wasn't wearing a bra was obvious, as her nipples were showing through and it was like her breasts were thumbing their noses at all the men in the room. She had a worldliness about her, a subtle hardness in the unlined face that let you know she was older than she at first appeared, that she was a broad over thirty stuck with a lovely but incongruous sixteen-year-old Lolita of a face.

I wanted her.

But then so did every other man in the place, and some of the women too, I supposed. I shrugged to myself and looked around and saw the sign over the double push doors to the left of the bar saying, "To Bunny's Lounge." I walked through the doors and into the anteroom and on to the lounge, and it was like walking into another dimension.

The lounge was all reds and browns, the lights low and red-tinted, the walls brown-paneled wood, the carpet a lush, soft red, soft to look at, soft to walk on. The tables in here were just as small but far more spread out, and set mostly for two, occasionally for four. An intimate room, for couples who wanted to be by themselves, maybe eat a quiet meal, sip a few drinks before slinking off to bed somewhere. There were a couple of couples going through such preliminaries right now. Otherwise I had the place to myself.

The kitchen was off to the back, and was probably nothing lavish. Anyway the menu wasn't, just a modest assortment of steaks, a few seafoods, a few sandwiches, all priced medium to medium high. The hostess, a pretty brunette in a dark pants suit, informed me when she seated me that it was too late in the evening to get a dinner, and nothing was now being served but sandwiches and of course cocktails. I ordered an open-face steak sandwich that came with french fries and iced tea and also ordered a gimlet.

I took my time with the food, enjoying the music that was being piped in, Ramsey Lewis-type low-key jazzy Muzak, and only faintly could I hear the pulse of the rock going on in the other room. I sipped my gimlet and then sipped three more and I was feeling good when I left.

Back in the anteroom I stood in my happy glow and happened to notice the wall facing me. I hadn't seen it when I first came through, as it had been to my back, but the wall was covered by framed pictures. I studied them and realized why the place was called Bunny's. The pictures were of a pretty, well-built blonde greeting people at the door of one of the Playboy Clubs, with one double-frame showing off two pages from an old *Playboy*, from one of their "Bunnies of Chicago" spreads. The pretty blonde was in two pictures at the bottom of the double-page spread, one of them in her Bunny threads greeting, another a discreet nude pose, with the girl in bed, mostly covered and wrapped in pink sheets, though one exposed breast, also pink, peeked out at the side. The write-up between the pictures described the blonde as "Pert Peg Baker, cornfed gal from Port City, a dot on the Iowa map," and went on to say the twenty-year-old girl had gone to high school and junior college in her home town, then trekked to the big city for fame and fortune. The spread came from a *Playboy* of at least a decade ago, and I vaguely remembered seeing it then. The blonde in the picture was, as you've guessed, that same blonde who was sitting aloof in the bar, and was no doubt the exception to the you-can't-come-home-again rule, as this ex-Bunny had made something out of her small potatoes *Playboy* fame and fortune.

So I went out to take another long look at her, where she still sat in the corner, watching the combo drummer. I found a stool at the bar and kept watching. I was working a beer down in there among the gimlets and a voice said, "She's something, isn't she?"

I looked at him. He was around thirty, kind of bland-looking, short hair, sportcoat; like me, he was one of the few business-types in the crowd. I said, "Huh?"

He said, "I said, uh, she sure is something."

"She's something."

"You passing through Port City?"

"Yeah."

"Salesman?"

"Yeah."

"Me too." He gulped at his beer and nodded toward the blonde. "I asked around about her."

"Oh."

"She owns this place. Her and another guy own it, anyway."

"I figured that."

"Oh, you saw the pictures?"

"Yeah."

"Good-looking chick. I'd sure like to get some of that."

"Why don't you try?"

"Already did."

"Oh."

"Zilch, man. Struck out royal."

"A shame."

"Yeah, and they told me she puts out."

"Maybe she's particular."

"Guess with her looks she can afford to be particular."

"Looks like she's got a man," I said, gesturing toward

the stage where the band was playing. "For tonight anyway."

"Yeah, the drummer, yeah I noticed her looking at him. She and him were talking during the break, When I asked around about her they said she likes younger guys." He paused. "Hell, I'm just thirty-one. You figure that's old?"

"No."

"But I guess it isn't young either. Hell. She's nice."

"She's nice all right."

"Younger guys, sheesh. She looks young herself, to me."

"Not if you look close."

"Yeah?"

"Yeah."

"Well I guess she would be in her thirties at that. Those Bunny pictures were from a while back."

"Right."

"Whatever, she's nice. Nice stuff."

"Nice stuff."

"Well. I'll see you."

"See you."

The guy finished his beer and took off and I stood and watched her some more. I never did get eye contact with her. I wondered if she knew I was watching. I ordered another beer. I wondered if I could get near her. I wondered if that was wise, considering she was probably real well-known around town. I nibbled at the beer. I wondered how she was in bed.

13

I woke up the next morning around noon, a sour film lining my mouth, a sour mood lining my brain. The hangover was heavy in me, like thick fluid, and that irritated me. And the bed I woke up in was my own, and that irritated me too. Last night my goal had been to get drunk and laid, and while one out of two may not be bad, tell that to a guy the morning after. The night before, however, had been something else again. I came home to the YMCA, feeling no pain but still the captain of my own ship—well, first mate, anyway. My hormones were pretty much in check from my bout with Helen what's-her-name back at the Howard Johnson's yesterday, and I'd gotten a certain satisfaction out of just standing and mentally feeling up Bunny of Bunny's. I don't think Boyd crossed my mind once, or the mark, Albert Leroy, either. Not right then anyway.

To show you how much in control I was, I managed to remember there was no can in my room, that my only source for relief was the communal john on the Y's dormitory floor where mine and all the other "apartments" were. My bladder was near explosion point and as I pushed open the door and flicked on the light switch, I heard a chorus of voices say, "Hey!" "Watch it!" "What the fuck!"

Automatically I flicked the light switch back off and was wheeling back out the door, my mind clouded but alert enough to know something stunk in Denmark. If I carried a gun, I might've reacted real bad. But I don't, so I didn't.

Then I got the picture. Quite literally.

On the wall of the large john-room were the silvery, flickering images of a film. A woman in a dark wig and nothing else was sitting on the edge of a bed; she had fleshy thighs and was spreading them, bountiful droopy breasts staring downward at the action. There was no sound, other than that of the eight-millimeter projector clicking and clacking away and some scattered hard breathing from the audience, which I gathered was made up of five or six fellow YMCA residents. Sitting on the floor of the can of the Young Men's Christian Association, digging the porno.

I laughed and went back outside, getting my key from out my pocket. I was almost down to my room when I heard a voice from behind me say, "Hey man! Hey, Johnson!"

That was the name I was registered under. I turned and said, "Yeah?"

It was the bearded guy, the youngish Gabby Hayes who had checked me in. And by young I mean somewhere between twenty-five and forty, don't ask me where.

"Say, man," he said, "go on back in the john and do what you have to."

I laughed again and said, "Never mind. You boys scared the piss right out of me."

"That doesn't offend you, does it?"

"Offend me?"

"Those pornies, I mean. Look, everybody here on the floor knows about it, and I only show 'em because the guys enjoy it. They pitch in and I send for the stuff in the mail. From the back of the men's mags. I don't hardly make a cent on it, honest to Christ."

"Hey. No big deal."

"No, but it is. I'd get fired if anybody reported this. If any of the guys staying here don't approve, fine, I'll stop showing 'em. So if you don't like it, please say so, okay?"

"Listen, I don't really care one way or the other."

He smiled, nodded his shaggy head. "You're all right, Johnson."

"Thanks. Look, I wouldn't mind taking a shower before I turn in. How much longer does the Bijou go on in there?"

"Should be over in five minutes. Can you hold out that long?"

"Sure."

"Look, I'll come down to your room and knock when I've got everybody out of the john, okay?"

I nodded.

Ten minutes later I was sitting on the bed, shoes off, rubbing my feet, and the knock came at the door. I got up and opened it and Gabby said, "All clear."

"Fine."

"You wouldn't care for a nightcap, would you?"

If I hadn't been drunk, it might've occurred to me that maybe this guy had in him some of what Boyd was. But I was drunk. So I said, "I already had more than I need, but…what the hell."

"Fine. Come on."

He had a bottle of whiskey, I didn't notice what kind, which he poured over ice from a little cooler he kept in one corner of his room. He used water glasses and poured them three-quarters full; a refill would be unnecessary. I sat at the chair at the desk-dresser and he sat on the bed.

"Thanks for understanding about the movies."

"Okay."

"It's not that I'm a sex maniac or anything."

"Sure."

"Or those other guys either. It's just something to do."

"I understand."

"Do you?"

"Sure."

"You understand then. That's good. That's real good. Because I don't want anybody getting the wrong impression."

"Yeah."

"You a salesman, or what?"

"Yeah."

"You got a wife?"

"No."

"Girlfriend?"

"A few."

"More than one, huh? Girl in every port?"

"Here and there."

"Anything steady?"

"No."

"Take my advice. Get somebody steady. Listen to me. I'm older than I look, you know. I ran away from home when I was a kid."

I was too drunk to notice how contrite the guy was getting. If I'd looked at him close I probably would've seen tears in his eyes. But I didn't look at him.

I concentrated on my drinking and several minutes went by before I realized he'd been talking quite a while, talking about God knows what. He was saying, "…bummed around a long time. My folks were dead and buried before I ever got back home. I was bumming before it was popular. I hitchhiked when it was a way of life, not a damn fad. You know what I'm saying?"

"Sure."

"No you don't. You don't know what I'm saying. You don't know why I show movies to those guys either."

"Sure I do."

"No. You don't know why I asked you for a drink."

"Yeah I do."

"What then?"

"You don't want to lose your job. You want to make sure I'm okay."

"You're okay, I know you're okay. That's maybe part of it, I guess, making sure you're okay, but you still don't know, do you?"

"Sure I do."

"You're a salesman, you say?"

"Yeah."

"How long?"

"Five years."

"You're young yet. You thirty?"

"No."

"You're young yet. Get another job."

"What?"

"Get off the road."

"What?"

"Find somebody. Find some woman. Or somebody."

"Sure."

"I mean it. If you don't, you know what happens?"

"No."

"You mean you don't know?"

"Tell me."

"You wake up old."

"Is that right?"

"That's right. And you find yourself old and alone and in a room and you die that way."

I looked at him. For a moment he was Albert Leroy. Sitting on that bed and wearing a gray sweater with diamond shapes on it. For an icy instant he was my mark.

I blinked.

Hard.

And I looked again and he was a young Gabby Hayes. Only he didn't seem so young anymore, and I didn't feel so drunk anymore.

I thanked him for the whiskey and left the room.

So I went to bed depressed and woke up with a sour film in my mouth and a sour mood in my mind and I climbed out of bed and took the shower I never got around to the night before and went down for a long, cold swim.

I had to see Boyd today. Had to. Today was Wednesday —and Thursday was the day.

14

The pool was long and narrow. The water was green to look at and cool to swim in. Cool was good. I hate it when the water's overheated, it puts me off—it's closer to soaking in a big hot bath than swimming in a pool.

For a long time I swam. Somewhere between one hour and two. A good half hour of that was spent floating on my back and staring at the ceiling and thinking. It wasn't good to think. Not on a job, not when your mind should be uncluttered. But if thinking couldn't be helped, best to do so in a relaxed way like this.

I loved the water. Its coolness, its gentle, lazy movement. The water made me think of Wisconsin, even though this water was full of chlorine and in Wisconsin the water was clear and fresh. I thought of Wisconsin and the lake and the nice moments my life had its share of.

My life.

I thought about it, defined it: *I live in a small A-frame, a prefab, on a lake in Wisconsin. Alone. I'm within an easy drive of Lake Geneva, where I belong to the Playboy Club, where I spend a night or two a week, when I'm not working. One night a week I play cards with some friends of mine down at Twin Lakes, mostly old guys who've retired, doctors and dentists and lawyers who stay the year round, though the crowd changes during the summer and the winter skiing months, when some men closer my age drift into the penny ante game. Once a year I go to Las Vegas and gamble and do my best to screw some pretty girls; sometimes I win. Once a year, in the winter, I go to Fort Lauderdale and soak up some sun. When I'm at the lake, in summer months, I swim and sun and water ski when I can find a knowledgeable female assistant to help me with my boat. There are many nice outdoor things to do around there in the fall, and the spring too, but in the winter I stay inside and listen to my stereo and watch television and read an occasional paperback western. When I'm not working.*

A nice life: *comfortable, better than comfortable. I work six, maybe seven jobs a year, for varying fees, my yearly income averages between fifteen and twenty thousand, a lot for a man alone, though I manage to spend every cent every year. I pay taxes on an income of seven or eight thousand, under my salesman cover; Broker fills out the IRS forms for me. My cover is something of a joke: door-to-door salesman of women's "personal wear," meaning hosiery and lingerie and the like. I still take along a sample case and credentials, but first year or so I took the case door-to-door some, establishing myself in whatever town the hit was in as a salesman, while Boyd was doing his lookout thing. Later I decided that was stupid. It was better to be invisible, and the cover was useless as far as cops were concerned anyway. After all, cops wouldn't ask questions till you did something, and the only thing you would do is kill some guy, immediately after which you'd be the hell out of town. And if they did happen to catch you in the act or something, a fuck of a lot of good a damn sample case of underwear is going to do you.*

"You mind if we join you, son?"

I got off my back to tread water and looked down toward the shallow section of the pool where a short, fat-bellied guy in his fifties, who was the one who'd spoken, and a short but skinny guy with white hair all over his chest and none on his head who was also in his fifties, were sloshing their way into the water. I stroked over to the side and climbed out.

I said, "All yours, gentlemen. I was just getting out."

The fat one nodded and grinned and the two men lolled around in the shallow end like a couple overage water babies.

There was an exercise room downstairs. I found it empty, which was the way I hoped to find it. Empty of people that is: the room had plenty of equipment, such as barbells and wall-pulleys and chinning bar and rowing machine. I spent a long time in there. Sweat rolled off my body and got the bad things in me out. I exercised mechanically, with speed and concentration, with a pleasant mindlessness that was just what I needed right then.

But when I started to get tired the thinking hit me again. I was on the rowing machine and I got to thinking about Boyd and Broker and my job and how long was it all going to last, anyway?

I was spoiled, maybe, from five years of smooth runs,

five years of nothing-goes-wrong and then all of a sudden Boyd loses his edge and almost gets me killed last job. Then Broker pulls that half-ass, last-minute airport deal on me, where it's not enough I off the guy, I got to play strong-arm and delivery boy too. By that Broker betrayed the trust I had in him and our working arrangement.

Your mind works things out sometimes. Your subconscious, I mean. In my mind somewhere I knew that if I ever wanted to quit doing what I was, I ought to have some money laid aside to fall back on. But I didn't: I had spent every nickel and that was something I never faced. But my subconscious did. My subconscious made me hold onto half that load of heroin. My subconscious was responsible for me having that little key to that little locker forty miles away at the Quad City Airport. A locker that had a bag of stuff in it that was my nest egg, my ticket out of Broker's loving arms, my everything. Till I found something else at least.

My subconscious had made a decision: *get the hell out. I've lost faith in Broker. And Boyd. This is it for me. Just this one damn dipshit little job. Just wipe out this one poor mark, this Albert Leroy who's dead on his feet anyway, and quit or disappear or whatever but get the hell out! No more Boyd, no more Broker, maybe quit the racket altogether. Maybe not. It isn't the killing. It's working with people I got no trust in is killing me.*

I got up off the rowing machine. In the corner was a punching bag. I went over to it and started hitting it, pretending it was Boyd, and suddenly I wasn't tired anymore and I hit it for a long while. I took out a lot of frustration on that bag, and when I was done I was tired again. But refreshed. To take the coat of sweat off I went back up to the pool, which was again empty of people, and swam for another half hour. I was alone the whole time. It was wonderful.

By the time I got back to my room it was five o'clock. On my way up to the room I'd stuck my head out of the air-conditioned Y and found that one of those late summer scorchers had come out of nowhere and descended on Port City. So I said to hell with the sportcoat-and-tie business and got myself a short-sleeve mock-turtleneck Ban-Lon and a pair of denim slacks from my suitcase and put them on. I felt like a human being again.

Down the street, near the waterfront, I found a restaurant that would feed me breakfast. I consumed several omelets and a lot of toast and bacon and I felt good by the time I got back to the Y. It takes a long while to get dark in the Midwest, thanks to Daylight Saving Time, so I sat downstairs in the small television room of the Y and watched a made-for-TV movie, and then it was nine o'clock and late enough to go calling on Boyd.

Boyd was sitting, back to wall, facing away from the window, a can of Bud between his legs. There was a smile under his mustache; he was enjoying the cool night breeze coming in the open window. His eyes were closed and he looked asleep, but as soon as I got within a few feet of him, he said, "Albert's having his soda right now. You can expect him to come out of the drugstore and start strolling back down the street, oh…" He checked his watch. "…three minutes from now."

"Hello, Boyd."

"Hello."

"It was hot today."

"Sure was."

"Did he wear his sweater?"

"No, by God he didn't. First time, too."

"Maybe he's human after all."

"But he did wear a long-sleeve shirt."

I shook my head and sat down on the davenport.

"Want me to get you a beer?" Boyd said.

"No."

"You know, I'm thinking of taking up permanent residence here. This apartment is something else."

"Sure is."

"Do you know that the fridge was full of beer and food, before I even got here?"

"No kidding."

"Sure was. Whoever our host is, he's thoughtful. And, shit, Quarry, you know what? Budweiser. That was what kind of beer was in it. My favorite kind, can you beat it?"

"You can't beat it."

"Listen, Quarry, I want to ask you something."

"Shouldn't you be watching?"

He made a face, half-turned toward the window. A couple minutes went by and he said, "Here comes the gink. Thirty seconds off schedule. Yeah. There he goes. Go to the door, gink. Thata boy. Fumble for your goddamn key. Thata gink, thata boy." Boyd belched and turned back to me. "Boring. We're doing the world a favor this time out."

"Are we."

"Sure."

"This guy's dead already, Boyd. Who wants a dead man killed?"

"That isn't our business. Our business is doing him."

"You're right. I think I'll go get myself a beer."

"Do that. Do that, Quarry."

A few minutes later I was sitting sipping the beer and Boyd said, "Quarry?"

"Yeah."

"I want to ask you something."

"Shoot."

"What you said last night."

"What did I say last night."

"You said, uh, you said maybe we been working together too long."

"Did I say that?"

"Yeah you sure as shit did. I mean, you didn't mean that, did you? We're a team, Quarry, a good one. It bothers me you saying that kind of thing."

"I must've been in a bad mood."

"That's an understatement. You didn't mean it, then?"

"I didn't mean it."

He grinned. "That's a relief. Whew! I'm telling you, I've had, well…a few problems in my, uh, personal life. I think I'm straightened out now, but it's been kinda rough, you know what I mean? I don't want to bring that into it, but I been feeling, sort of...well a person gets these feelings of rejection sometimes, you know? I know you don't like discussing personal matters and such, but I really like working with you, I consider you as more than just a working partner, I like to think of you as my friend. You know."

"We been together a long time."

"We sure have. I hope we'll be together a lot longer time, too."

"Me too, Boyd."

He nodded and kind of sighed and turned back and watched the window for a while. Then he swiveled around and said, "Look, I'd like to walk down to the taxicab stand and get something to read. You want to take over for me for a minute?"

"Sure. How long you be gone."

He stood. "Maybe an hour."

"How the hell far away is this taxicab stand, anyway?"

"Just down the block. But I like to look their books over good, you know, before I pick one out. I won't read just any old thing. And they got one of those sandwich machines, you heat 'em up in little plastic wrappers, you know?"

"One of those infrared deals."

"Right. So I thought I'd have a sandwich. So how about you take over for a while?"

"Sure."

"I appreciate it." He started to walk out of the room, stopped midway. "Quarry?"

"Yeah."

"You're all right."

"Sure."

"No, I really mean it. You're an all right guy."

"Thanks, Boyd."

"And I'm glad you said what you said, about not meaning what you said. Like you said, we been together a long time. With a long time yet to come, right?"

"Right," I said.

15

My eyes opened and focused and saw the face of a clock. Alarm clock, my little travel alarm on the nightstand by the bed. The clock had been set for four, which was how it read, and I looked at it not understanding why the bell wasn't going. Still half-asleep, I took the clock in my hands and examined it carefully and the bell rang and I jumped upright in bed, scared momentarily shitless.

I sat there for a second looking at and listening to the clock and tried to decide whether to swear or laugh and did neither. Instead I shut off the alarm and laid it back on the stand and climbed out of bed. I got a towel wrapped around me and walked down to the can to brush my teeth and take in a shower and shave. When I came back I put on a T-shirt and socks and sat back down on the bed.

From under the bed I pulled out the suitcase and briefcase and laid them open beside me. I drew my raincoat out of the suitcase and unfolded it and leaned over and draped the coat over the chair at the desk-dresser. Then I took the nine-millimeter automatic from the briefcase and removed the silencer. I cleaned and oiled the gun, then the silencer, though neither needed it, and also cleaned the spare barrel I'd be putting on the gun afterward. I reattached the silencer and returned gun and extra barrel to the briefcase and snapped it shut.

As I finished dressing, I went to the window and drew back the curtain. It was still dark out, though the corners of the sky were touched with a washed-out gray, about the color of the suit I was getting into. When I was dressed I looked at myself in the mirror, in my gray suit and black tie, and I could've been a businessman. A salesman maybe, like my cover. Or a pallbearer.

It was still dark when I got to Boyd's. I parked the Ford in front, three blocks down on the same street as Boyd and Leroy, leaving my briefcase and suitcase in the trunk. I had my raincoat over my right arm, the nine-millimeter stuck down in my belt. I walked around behind the building and used the stairs and found the door unlocked. Boyd was eating a grapefruit in the kitchen.

"Morning, Quarry."

"Morning."

"Want something to eat?"

"I don't eat before a job."

"Oh yeah, that's right. How do you feel?"

"Okay. Good. Fine."

Boyd got up from the table. He was in his T-shirt and boxer shorts. "Give me a second to get my clothes on."

"Hurry up."

"I will."

I laid my raincoat on the table and went over to the sink and got myself a glass of water and drank it and Boyd came back. I said, "Set to pull out?"

"Sure."

"You driving that green Mustang in back? In the alley there?"

"Yeah, that's right."

"I've seen that before. You drove it on the last job, too, didn't you?"

"Course I did, it's my car."

"Think that's wise?"

"You're getting fucking paranoid, Quarry."

"Maybe. Maybe I am."

"Oh, I almost forgot..." He dug in his pants pocket and got out a key and handed it to me.

I looked at the key and shook my head. "A key to the front door."

"Aw what's so strange about that, we've had it easy before."

"I didn't say it was strange."

"Bullshit, you been talking about what a strange job this was ever since you got here."

"I'm not talking now."

"Okay, all right, Quarry. Let's just do it and get out, huh?" Boyd sat back down at the table. "You be sure to mess things up good. You know. Rip the mattress up a little, why don't you? You got a knife?"

"Yeah."

"Good."

"I take it Mr. X made the drop okay."

"Fine, real fine. You want to see?"

"Okay."

Boyd got up and I followed him into the bedroom. He opened his suitcase and got out an envelope that had money in it. He rippled the edges of the bills and I nodded and he smiled.

"How much?" I said.

"Just shy two grand apiece," he said. He was playing with one corner of his mustache.

"That's a five-grand hit," I said. "Not the best money in the world, but this has got to be more important a job than it looks to us."

"If you want to ask Broker some questions, fine. Me, I'll take my money and run."

"Yeah. You're right, Boyd, it's not good thinking about a job like I been. Not good at all."

"You don't want to take your share with you now, do you?"

"Hell no. You think that would be smart?"

"I usually wouldn't, Quarry, but in this hick town what's the difference? Nobody's up yet, and you could just hop in your car and leave directly."

"No. I'll stop up for it right after."

"Well don't take your time getting back."

"Do I ever take my time getting back?"

"No."

"Okay then."

"Quarry."

"Yeah."

"You better get going, you want to get it done before light."

"I'm on my way."

"Do it, man."

"Right."

I stopped at the door and said, "Look, Boyd, this job has been a little, well…"

"Queer?" Boyd said, smiling a little. "Yeah, I guess it has. Not much we can do though, huh? Except do it."

"Well just the same, we better have a signal, in case something sours."

"Okay. His shade is up over cross the way. I'll be watching out the window, so if something goes wrong, pull the shade. Halfway down if I should get the hell out, say it's cops or something. Pull it all the way down if you need help. Okay?"

"Fine. Same signal goes for you, then."

"Fine."

I put on my gloves. I took the silenced automatic from out my belt and held it in my right hand and folded the raincoat over my arm, covering gun-in-hand. I said, "See you, Boyd."

"See you, Quarry."

He gave me a thumbs-up sign and I returned it and left.

The sky was almost light, if you can call a murky gray sky light, and between that and the still-burning street lamps, I didn't exactly have the cover of night to protect me. Not that it mattered: the street was empty, like a deserted movie backlot, and down half a block at the corner the traffic lights were going, changing colors as if to entertain themselves. So I wasn't upset when there was no back entrance to Albert Leroy's building. I had to use a street entrance, an unlocked door stuck between the taco joint and the laundry, but had no bad feelings about it.

The stairs creaked as I ascended, and I guess I would've bitched too if I was a hundred years old and somebody walked on me. The walls were flaking brown paint and the air was so musty I wanted to cough. When I got to the tiny landing I found two doors, one of them obviously leading up to the vacant apartment on the upper floor, the other bearing a slot with a yellowed card in it reading, "Albert Leroy."

I worked the key in the lock.

The door opened on the kitchen. The ceiling was high, the walls a yellowing white, the stained wooden cabinets a darkening yellow. The kitchen appliances were ancient —a stoop-shouldered Westinghouse refrigerator and a four-burner gas range, the kind you light—and a kitchen table with a speckled Formica top was showing age, its plastic-covered chairs having seen better days, and the linoleum on the floor was cracked here and there and was rolling up at the edges. But the kitchen was clean, hospital clean. It even smelled like a hospital, as though he used it for surgical work instead of cooking.

A doorless archway led into the living room. It was small, a live-in elevator, with wallpaper of a faded purple-flowered design, like the pattern on an old woman's dress, fitting in well with the furniture, which was drab and lifeless, the kind of stuff the elderly stick doilies on to hide the shabbiness. The only modern piece of furniture was a reclining chair back across from the portable TV and it was broken into a constant back-tilt, which didn't help the limited space of the room. The guy was a hoarder, obviously, as the room was somehow both cluttered and orderly, stacks of books everywhere, newspapers saved, piles of backdated *TV Guide*s on the television, a table with a stamp collection in progress, but everything seemed in its special, assigned position.

To the right was the bedroom.

The door was open and I could see him, sleeping there on the bed. Since it had been a hot night, he was sleeping only in his pajama bottoms, and on top of the covers. His arms were stretched out as if reaching and his mouth was open and he looked like a fountain in a park. He was breathing hard but he was not snoring, his face a putty mask, formless, puffy.

I stood in the doorway and looked at him for a moment. I didn't go in there with him because the bedroom was so small it made the living room seem gigantic. I was plenty close here in the doorway. Close enough to see that his chest was sunken and he had just the start of a potbelly and neither chest nor belly had a hair on it; he was hairless smooth like a baby and I suddenly wondered how old he was. I had thought of him as an old man, but he was smooth, unwrinkled, unused. The only solid indications of age were streaks of white in his sandy crewcut and deep creases in the checks of that putty face. On his left arm was a long and unsightly brown birthmark that was hairy and ran from his outer bicep down cross his elbow and twisting round almost to his wrist and I now knew the reason for cardigan sweaters and long-sleeve shirts in summer.

I thought I saw his eyes flicker open for a moment just after the gun made its snicking sound and the bullet went crushing through his sternum. But I wasn't sure. His body did a little dance, a small, quick jerk and that was all. His mouth stayed open, but slackly so, and he was limp, a stringless puppet.

It took two minutes to mess up the apartment. As I was doing it I knew it was illogical that anyone would try to rob this guy, but that was the way we'd been asked to handle it. I kicked his books around, knocked some chairs over, ripped up a few of the newspapers, tipped over the table with the stamps and magnifying glass and stamp book on it, dumped everything out of his hoarder's closet, which was more books, newspapers, magazines, letters, stamps, and other assorted junk, and spread it around. A dresser of clothes in the living room—no space for it in the bedroom—I emptied and then tipped over. I gutted the sofa with my pocketknife and when I was through I went into the bedroom, shoved him to one side and then my nostrils filled with the smell of blood and shit: his bowels had voided with his body's death. I made one quick obligatory rip down the center of the mattress and wiped the knife blade clean on a sheet and got the hell out of there. I shut the bedroom door behind me to keep the stink from crawling into the living room and I took a long breath of fresh air, sucking it into my lungs as it rolled in the open window. I took my raincoat from where I'd slung it over a chair, then set the chair down on its side to help the ransack effect. I folded the coat over my arm and glanced out the window. Light out there now, I noticed. It was dawn.

Then I noticed something else.

Across the way the shade was drawn.

16

Boyd's door was locked.

I got out a key and used it. I turned the knob and eased the door forward, just enough to see if it was night-latched. It wasn't. Good. I wouldn't have to break it open. I could go in quiet. Slow. Careful. I did.

I stood there in the kitchen, closing the door soundlessly behind me, getting my eyes accustomed to the blackness of the apartment. I never realized how very dark this apartment could be, this long boxcar of an apartment with its only source of natural light being windows on either end. Every electric light in the place was switched off and the shade was drawn in the kitchen.

As was the shade in the living room, of course.

A full minute passed and night vision gradually came to me and I got my bearings. The door from the kitchen to the bedroom was open and so was the door from bedroom to living room, and I could see Boyd down there by the shaded window, but just barely, just his outline, just a quiet mass of something sitting way down there at the end of the boxcar.

I listened.

I listened and tried to hear a sound, any sound, any indication that someone else was in this damn apartment besides me, Boyd and silence.

And heard nothing.

I didn't know what had gone wrong, but I knew it wasn't likely to be law. If cops had somehow got wind of us and had come barging in (which was goddamn unlikely in Port City) Boyd would have pulled the shade halfway down, rather than down full, to signal me to get the hell away. If it was cops he wouldn't signal help. Or he shouldn't, anyway. Most likely it was something else. I didn't know what. But it was something…someone…else.

I didn't waste time thinking about who. A joker had turned up in the game and nobody mentioned anything about wild cards but I had to play the hand anyway. So. I went carefully forward, holding my gun arm tight against my ribcage, my wrist bent into a ninety-degree angle so that the nine-millimeter was pointing straight out, ready to blast anything, any damn thing that moved.

Nothing moved.

At least, nothing moved here in the kitchen. And there was no good place to hide in here, really, other than in the closet that housed the furnace, and that afforded only a narrow cubbyhole barely large enough for a child to squeeze into. I got close enough to see that the door to the furnace closet was open and the cubbyhole empty and I moved on.

The living room, I remembered, had no good hiding places, either. No furniture in corners that could shelter a hiding man, except possibly if someone should hide down behind the far end of the davenport that was against the wall on the right, near that window where

Boyd was silently sitting; but the davenport sat so low to the ground that a man would have to curl in a ball to hide, which doesn't make for the best of ambush techniques. And too, if Boyd was alive, quietly waiting to make a stand, the intruder wouldn't be anywhere near him; likewise if Boyd was dead, the intruder wouldn't want to be close at hand—even a pro (if this *was* a pro) doesn't like being next door to a corpse, not for long anyway. The living room I ruled tentatively out, though admittedly that was where the front entrance was, the door being over on the left, near the back corner, and someone could be behind that door, waiting out on the landing. But I doubted that. I figured once the intruder got *that* far, got out the door and close to freedom, he'd most likely take off. Unless his express purpose was to kill Boyd and me, and since I didn't know the intruder's motives, yet, I had to count that as a possibility.

But not the best one.

The best possibility was the bedroom, which had two excellent vantage points for surprise attack: a large closet with sliding double doors and room enough for five men to hide; and a bathroom in the left corner on the left side, a small bathroom but one with a shower-curtained tub.

The odds were good, very good, that I'd find my intruder either in the bedroom or in the bathroom that led off from it.

I unfolded my raincoat, took it by the collar and shook it gently and held it in front of me and it was like a man was looking back at me. I walked slowly over to the open

door to the bedroom and eased my hand around the
corner to flick on the light switch, flooding the room with
light, and tossed in the coat.

No reaction.

Well.

I moved into the room in a low crouch, fanning the
gun around, looking, looking, looking.

Empty.

The fucking room was empty.

The double doors on the closet had been slid down to
one end and a lot of hangers were staring me in the face.
I walked over slow, staying low, and slid the doors back
the other way, fast, and saw more hangers.

Okay.

The bathroom, then.

If the bathroom was empty, then whoever had caused
Boyd's trouble, whatever it was, had gotten away before I
got there. Or was waiting in the living room. I couldn't
forget that; if the bathroom was empty I still wasn't home
free. I stood in the doorway of the can and tried to flick
on the light but the switch clicked forth and back impo-
tently, the bulb evidently burned out. I turned to the tub
with its shower curtain and reached out and began tentatively to draw back the curtain and something lashed out,
something solid, something much more solid than a fist,
doubled me over, something metal had creased my belly
and folded me in half like a slice of bread and I looked
through burning eyes as a dark mass rose from the bottom
of the tub, looked with red eyes into the black T-shirt of
the man who'd hit me, who was now on his feet in the tub

and I saw and heard a swishing object as it came down. I jerked to the left, collided with a wall and saw from the corner of my eye the object, a wrench, go sinking into my shoulder, making a crunching sound as it went, and I was down on my knees, like I was praying, my spine jammed hard against the stool behind me, and an arm swinging the wrench came down after me. With my free hand I batted upward and knocked the arm away before it did me any more damage and brought up my automatic and fired and the silenced gun went *chunk*; and *chunk* again, sounding loud in the confines of the small room, and I heard a yelp. I didn't see him, not really, didn't know for sure if the gun had hit home, but the wrench-swinger was scared, so shitass helpless scared, he started in waving his arms and got us tangled in the shower curtain somehow, and fabric and metal rods were down on us, and I fired again, hoping my gun wasn't aimed at some part of me, and the man with the wrench, still scared, more scared, didn't finish me like he could have, like he should have, but scrambled out of there, tucked tail between legs and left in a blur of black.

I thought he flicked off the bedroom light switch as he went out, because everything went dark, but when I woke up I realized it was minutes later, how many I didn't know, not many, that was for sure, but by the time I was on my feet and staggering after the man with the wrench, he was gone. Not long gone maybe, but gone long enough. In the kitchen the door was wide open and when I got to the fire-escape porch there was no sight of anybody.

I shut the kitchen door, locked it. I stumbled over to

the cupboard, got out a bottle of aspirin and shook out six and got a glass of water from the tap and gulped down pills and water and stood there leaning on the counter, panting. Then I went to the kitchen table and sat down for a moment and stroked my crushed left shoulder with my right hand and felt tears run down my face and said, "Jesus Christ," a few times, and then I ran fingers across my clavicle and it was fucked up, too, fucked over bad.

When my mind stopped being red with pain, it got red with anger and I slammed my fist down on the table and barely felt the pain as it shot back through my shoulder. By the time I was on my feet again, maybe a second later, I'd forgotten about the pain.

Back in the bedroom I found Boyd's suitcase in a corner, open, flung there after it had been dumped out.

I went through the pile of clothes and the envelope was gone. I glanced in a wastecan and found it: the envelope had been emptied and then crumpled into a tight ball. I looked around the room for a while, but only for a very short while, as a search was useless. It was something I had to face: the money was gone.

What I found in the living room was no surprise.

Boyd was in his usual position at the window: sitting on the floor; leaning against the wall; head tilted back; but dead. The upper side of his head was caved in and looked as though it had been gently done, as though his was the head of a china doll that had been delicately shattered with a single tap of a child's hammer. But maybe that was because it was dark in there. Maybe if I had had to look at him closer, in the light, I would have seen it the way it was: a man's skull cracked bloody open from two or more savage blows of a hard-swung wrench. His eyes were round open and glowing white in the blackness and I could almost hear his voice speaking in those dead eyes, *Quarry...Quarry, what the fuck?* The reality of death must've been a shock to Boyd, the cruelty, the absurdity, the finality, the million things that must flash through your mind as you die violently. A man can get detached on the winning side of a gun and he can forget what it is he's doing and Boyd, evidently, died in a traumatic realization of what he was, what he did and what was being done to him. But at least he'd shown one last trait of professionalism, in his final moment: his right hand was still clutching the shade he'd pulled down to warn me.

I had to give him that much.

17

Under the wooden steps in back, grouped close against the wall, were garbage cans. Six of them. I arranged them into a slight semicircle and that was where I left Boyd.

My shoulder was a hunk of agony and made it no pleasure carrying my ex-associate down those three flights of steps. But it had to be done. I didn't know if the Port City cops would buy this as what was perhaps a rare event around these parts—a mugging—but that's what I was hoping. I had stripped Boyd of all valuables, leaving his pockets pulled inside out, not only to fabricate a robbery, but to prevent discovery of Boyd's identity. With luck, Boyd would end up just another cipher in a potter's field, a poor slob who was passing through Port City and got mugged and killed for his trouble.

I hadn't had the time to analyze what had happened yet and was acting, really, out of sheer instinct: I was a knee struck by a mallet at the precise point and was jerking up like I was supposed to. Reflex had me getting Boyd out of there and away from that apartment, which had been provided by our nameless employer, who by unwritten law must be protected at all costs. Or almost all: it would have been better to lug Boyd off someplace farther away, like drive him out along the Mississippi twenty miles and dump him off a bluff, but I wouldn't take that big a chance. Reflex action or not, confusion or no, I thought of my ass first. Survival.

So I had cleaned both Boyd and apartment of his effects and placed everything I collected in the trunk of his green Mustang. I had wrapped Boyd in a sheet, which I removed once I deposited him behind the wall of cans, and had slung him over my good shoulder and headed down the fire escape, hoping for the best.

I was lucky about the configuration of the alley, which in fact wasn't really an alley at all, as it dead-ended halfway in, surrounded by three-story buildings, making for something of a modest courtyard back there. The windows in the buildings were few and as yet dark—it was still very early morning—and the building across the way was a garage and windowless. The dreary buildings and the overcast sky gave me a perhaps false sense of security, and once I had pulled Boyd's Mustang up into the mouth of the street entry, blocking it off and partially obstructing vision from out there, I felt relatively safe carrying him down. Or as safe as you can feel in the company of somebody murdered.

I guided the Mustang out of the little courtyard and let loose a monumental sigh as I got out onto the still empty street. As I drove around to the front the street lights winked out, officially signaling morning's arrival, and I pulled the Mustang into a vacant spot behind my gray rental Ford and turned the car off and sat there for a while. Across the street all was silent. No one had stumbled onto

Albert Leroy as yet. Idle curiosity made me wonder who would be found first—Boyd or Albert.

That particular irrelevant thought was a sign of just how dazed I was. I got out of the car and walked down to the corner and stood there for maybe a minute, alone on the sidewalk, gathering my thoughts. My mind had been blown, almost literally, and I didn't know how long it would take to collect the pieces and reassemble them.

Across the street, kitty-corner from where I stood, was a telephone booth, standing in front of a big gothic-looking church like a reminder of what century it was. The moment I saw it I was on my way over, digging a dime out of my pocket, searching for more change to make the necessary long-distance call.

"Hello," a voice said. A slightly groggy voice.

"Is this Carl?"

"Yes…yes it is. Who is this?"

"Get Broker's ass out of bed, Carl."

"Uh, who is calling please?"

"Get him out of bed, you fucking gimp."

"Quarry?"

I said nothing.

He said, "Okay, uh, okay, wait a second."

"Just."

It took three minutes.

Broker said, "Trouble?"

"Yes."

"Can you talk?"

"Yes."

"Are you sure?"

"I'm in a pay phone."

"Fine. What's the number?"

I told him.

"I'll need five minutes," he said, "to get to where I can talk."

"Okay."

I hung up.

Five minutes later, give or take ten seconds, the phone rang and I picked it off the hook and Broker said, "Go."

"Boyd's dead."

"How?"

"Somebody creamed him with a wrench."

"What about the job?"

"The job went all right. I came back to Boyd's right after and found him with his head smashed in. I had a scuffle with who did it, got my shoulder banged up a little, but nothing serious."

"You saw him then?"

"The guy who did it? No. It was dark and he hit me before I knew what was coming."

"No idea who or why?"

"I know why, I guess. Not who."

"Why then?"

"The money was gone."

"I see. This all just happened?"

"Within the past half hour."

"The authorities?"

"Nobody's seen either one of the bodies yet."

"Nobody but you."

"That's right."

"You cleaned up the mess?"

"Yeah." I told him what I had done, how I'd faked the mugging with Boyd, removed his things from the apartment.

"Good man, Quarry."

"What about Boyd? Can his body lead the law anywhere?"

"Not if you stripped him clean. His prints aren't on file anywhere. He wasn't even in the service, his homosexuality kept him free of that."

"No homo arrests? Child molesting or anything?"

"No. Boyd was gay, but conservative. You know me well enough to know I don't take on anybody unstable."

"Broker."

"Yes?"

"I'm getting an idea."

"What kind of idea?"

"An idea of who wasted Boyd."

"Who?"

"Who else? Our employer. The man who came to you and said he wanted Albert Leroy dead."

"Impossible."

"Possible. Very possible, for a number of reasons. Do I have to go into them, Broker?"

"No."

"Who is he, Broker?"

"I can't tell you that. You know I can't tell you that."

"Sure you can."

"Against policy."

"There you go again, Broker, talking like this is an insurance company and you're the president and I'm your top salesman."

"Is it really so different?"

"Christ, Broker!"

"This is a business and there are certain rules. You're asking me to break our most sacred trust."

"Sacred? Trust?"

"I can't tell you, Quarry. I won't tell you."

"Broker."

"No way, Quarry."

"I want my money."

"It's gone. Live with it."

"That's what I want to do, Broker. I want to find my money and live with it."

"I'll tell you what, Quarry."

"What?"

"I'll let you have the twenty-five percent down payment that was left with me. My commission. I'll hand it over to you. As a present. A bonus, let's say. But give this a rest."

"No."

"You're being unreasonable."

"Am I? I don't care if you give me the equivalent of all the money, my share, your share, Boyd's share. I want to find the bastard responsible. I want to make him eat that wrench."

"Maybe we should talk when you've calmed down."

"Okay, then. Call me back next year."

I hung up.

Thirty seconds later the phone rang again and I picked it up.

Broker said, "What do you intend to do?"

"I'm going to find out who hired me, Broker. If you won't tell me, I'll find out on my own."

"Jesus Christ! You're insane, man!"

"Impossible. You only work with stable personalities."

"Listen. Listen to me. Get out of that town. Get out. Now."

"I think I'll stay a while."

"Have you cracked up? You can't hang around after a job, especially one that's gone sour like this one has."

"Watch me."

"I'm going to tell you only one more time..."

"Good. Then I won't have to hear it anymore after that."

"...get out of Port City, Quarry."

"This isn't Chicago, Broker. This is a hick town and I'm not going to have any trouble."

"You're right, Port City isn't Chicago, you could *hide* in Chicago. In Port City you'll be conspicuous as hell."

"Goodbye, Broker."

"Wait!"

I waited.

"Isn't there anything I can say?"

"Sure."

"What?"

"The name of the guy who wanted Albert Leroy dead."

"Quarry, I'm not going to stand for this."

"Yes you are."

"All right. All right, all right, all right, make a fool of yourself, but Quarry…make damn sure none of it touches *me*. If you do that, if you even come close to endangering me, you know what I'll do."

"I know what you'll try to do."

"You aren't the only assassin in the world, Quarry."

"No. But how many do you have better?"

I hung up.

I sat there for thirty seconds and when the phone rang again I picked it up and said, "Hello, Broker."

"Quarry!"

"What, Broker?"

"Uh, what about Boyd's car?"

"What about it?"

"You've got to get rid of it."

"How?"

"Bring it up here and we'll get rid of it for you."

"I'm not sure I want to do that, Broker. I'm going to be kind of busy today."

"I tell you what…let me do some checking. I'll contact the man you're looking to find, I'll talk to him and try to find out if he knows anything. Give me till tonight and if I haven't got anything for you, go ahead, go ahead tomorrow and snoop all you want."

"I don't know, Broker."

"Trust me."

"Trust you. Kind of a sacred trust, huh, Broker?"

"Do you know the river road?"

"That old road that runs along the Mississippi, up to Davenport."

"Yes. There's a limestone quarry about ten miles outside of Davenport on the river road. Carl and I will be pulled alongside there at, say, midnight. Bring Boyd's car and at that time I'll tell you how I've done with…the man you want to find."

"How will I get back to Port City, Broker?"

"I'll have Carl drive you back. We'll bring two cars."

"Okay."

"Tonight, then? At the stone quarry?"

"Sure."

"I'll see you tonight, then."

"Sure."

"At midnight."

"Sure. See you then."

"See you then. Quarry?"

"Yeah?"

"Take care of yourself, will you? Lie low today and just take it easy."

"That's sweet, Broker. Your concern is goddamn fucking touching."

He hung up.

So did I.

18

The sign said "Coke" and underneath, in only slightly larger letters, "Port City Taxi Service," but the place was more than that: it was an all-night grocery of sorts, as well as restaurant and bookstore. The groceries ran to pretzels, pop and milk, and the books ran to porno paperbacks and skin mags, and the restaurant was little more than a couple of tables stuck next to a stand that had on it a coffeepot and napkins and plastic spoons and an infrared mini-oven for the heating of cellophane-wrapped sandwiches which were for sale at the counter as you came in.

Behind the glassed counter, which was long and full of candy and cigarettes, was a heavyset woman of indeterminate age with frowzy gray-brown hair and a curiously friendly face. She was wearing a red-and-white checkered dress that looked like a tablecloth left over from a 1957 picnic and was sitting in the corner with her back to an ancient black metal sender-receiver, a squared hand mike leading out from it on a worn spiral rubber cord and resting in one of her hands, a mostly smoked cigarette in the other. From somewhere out of the radio outfit came muffled static which she apparently understood, as she responded to it now and then.

When she and the static had finished talking to each

other, she grinned at me and said, "Howdy, mister. Little early yet, ain't it?"

"Sure is," I said.

"It gets early every morning round this time." She rasped out a little laugh and pointed a finger down toward the end of the counter. "Fresh rolls down there, dime a piece. You get first pick today, sonny. Early bird catches the worm. The coffee's still perking, shouldn't be more'n a couple of minutes and it'll be ready. There's a dish on the stand, by the napkin container. Drop a nickel in the dish for every cup of coffee you drink."

"Thanks."

I lifted the sheet of white paper on the box and looked in at rows of fresh, well-iced danish rolls and picked several out and left the old lady a quarter on the counter. I walked back and sat down at one of the tables and nibbled at a roll while I waited for the coffee.

The place was all length and little width, the groceries crowded on shelves on one side of the room, a few tall skinny glass-doored refrigeration units backed up flat against the wall like men in the St. Valentine's Day Massacre, and the paperbacks and magazines were thick on the other side of the room, various sorts of racks rubbing shoulders with one another. The ceiling was high and had all the room's breathing space to itself; the ceiling edges were curved, ornately sculpted with little nude cupids and such and vines and flowers, and I wondered how old the building was and what it once had been.

I sat and stared at the tarnished aluminum coffeepot

and listened to it perking. My mind was doing the same thing: perking, playing with thoughts, trying to get ready.

I didn't understand, yet, what exactly the occurrences of this still early morning added up to. My mind was fuzzy, the events floating around inside my head like the synthetic snow in a wintery paperweight. I didn't know what would happen next. I wasn't sure what had happened so far. But I did know what I was going to do.

I was going to find the man.

The man who had paid to have Albert Leroy killed.

Who else in Port City knew Boyd and I were in town? Who else in Port City knew Boyd would have thousands of dollars in a suitcase in that particular apartment on this particular morning?

Motivation? I had no idea of what motivation lurked behind all of this. In the first place, it was still a mystery to me how anyone could feel it necessary to have Albert Leroy killed. He wasn't my idea of the kind of man who posed a threat. Motivation, I didn't know about that. Yet.

The coffee was ready and I got myself a cup. I sipped it slowly and thought some more.

What about Broker? He knew about Albert Leroy and Port City and all of it; hell, he set it up. Was this some kind of Broker Machiavellian kiss-off?

Unlikely. If Broker wanted to get rid of a man he wouldn't do so in so sloppy a fashion, and in Broker's home territory. There are plenty of methods, far better ones, for weeding out your bad stock. If Broker wanted me dead, he'd send someone up to see me between jobs, when I was sitting on my ass, fishing in Wisconsin or something. I'd be found floating in the lake up there, if I was found at all, not in an apartment in Port City, across the street from where I'd just hit a man.

Of course I was well aware that Broker meant to stop me, at all costs, from playing Sherlock Holmes in Port City. I knew that the meeting tonight at that stone quarry (which could've been the very place that provided Broker the inspiration for the name he'd bestowed on me years back) would be in one way or another designed to get me out of this, out of the area, out of the situation, *out*. Just what extent of violence he had in mind for me, if any, I didn't know. I doubted Broker would try to have me killed, but it was possible. Possible.

It wasn't smart to stay in Port City, I knew that. But it wasn't smart to leave, either. In my business you have to know what's happening, where you stand, what exactly's being done to you and who by. I didn't want to leave Port City till I understood what had happened this morning. All I knew now was that someone had tried to kill me, and it wasn't smart to leave Port City till I knew who and why.

I also knew it wasn't risky, particularly, to stay in town, as long as I didn't stick around very long, long enough to give even hick town cops a chance to put the pieces together. If I could do it fast, in a day, maybe two, there was nothing to worry about. I had my salesman credentials and sample case if anyone asked questions at me hard, a cover that would hold water if it was checked out. As long as I didn't attract too much attention or act too overly cautious about my actions, suspicions weren't likely to be aroused. Soon as I left here, I would change barrels on the gun, toss the old barrel wrapped in the gloves I'd worn down a sewer duct, so nothing to worry about there.

There were logical answers to all the questions that came to my mind, and I answered them, all the while thinking: *I don't need reasons for what I do. No excuses, no logic. I do what feels right. I feel like I was double-crossed by the guy who hired me, and I feel like doing something about it.*

The door slammed up front and I looked up. A skinny guy in jeans and a white T-shirt walked over to the counter and slammed down his coin changer and tossed some bills down. "Checkin' in," he said. His voice was high-pitched and didn't fit the lean but tough look he carried with him, mostly coming from a dark complexion and scruffy black hair and a chipped-tooth smile.

"Where you been?" the old woman said. "Tried to get you on the call box."

"Some ol' bitch had me drive her home out in the country and I had to carry some shit in the house for her. She tipped me a goddamn quarter, you believe it, shee-it."

He came over, grabbing a couple of danish rolls, and got himself some coffee and sat down with me at the table and said, "Care if I sit down here with you, Jack?"

"You already are."

"Thanks, don't mind if I do."

He sat there and yelled up to the old lady, bantered back and forth with her, laughing over in-jokes, and the smell of him and his eating mouth-open while talking and the inane boring chatter got old fast. I got up and walked back to the book racks and looked them over.

One rack of paperbacks seemed largely devoted to gay literature and I recognized *Twilight Love*, a book I'd seen Boyd reading the other day, among the various titles and smiled for a moment and for that moment thought about Boyd and how before lately he hadn't been that bad of a guy.

The skinny cabbie came over carrying a half-eaten danish and poked me in the ribs with his elbow and winked and said, "Like that stuff, honey?"

His voice seemed effeminate now. I didn't know whether he was putting it on or not. For a second there I got mad—I don't really know why—and I looked at him straight on and cold and didn't say anything but he got the point. He was dumb, but he was smart enough to know I was going to hurt him if he said anything else.

After he went away I left the rack of books and headed for the magazines, then noticed a stack of papers in the corner, back by the Coke cooler. I walked over and bent down and took a look at them. Davenport papers, daily *Times*. They went back several days. Just for the hell of it I thumbed through them till I found notice of the airport death of a few days ago.

Floyd Feldstein, the guy's name had been. He was a buyer associated with Quad City Art Sales, Inc., which was a front of Broker's. There was no mention that he'd been dressed as a priest, or that he was carrying airline tickets made out in someone else's name. The Chief of Police stated that, after preliminary investigation, it was assumed that Feldstein had been robbed and killed by one of the "long-haired undesirables who have been seen of late frequenting our public places during off hours, presumably in the hopes of gaining ready cash for the purchase of illegal drugs." Well, something like that, Chief.

I walked back up to the table and got myself another cup of coffee and sat and drank it. It seemed like the more hot coffee I drank, the less my shoulder hurt. So I sat and sipped and thought.

Tonight, I decided, tonight I'm going to have to be careful.

Tonight, Broker. I'll see you tonight.

Today I've got other things to do.

19

Along the side wall of the Port City Taxi building, in the
open area between building and filling station next door,
was a long row of parking spaces, two of them filled by
taxis, five by other cars, a number of them vacant. The
upper wall was a triple billboard advertising toothpaste,
cigarettes, and a politician, but below that, hanging low
but visible, was a large sign saying, "Private Parking," in
big black block letters, with the usual warning of "Illegally
Parked Cars Towed Away at Owner's Expense" in strident,
no-nonsense red. The bottom lines of the sign, in business-
like black, said, "For Weekly, Monthly and Yearly Rates,
Inquire at Taxi Stand Desk." For ten dollars, the lady in
the red-and-white checkered dress behind the counter
was only too happy to provide a week's space for one
automobile and she asked no embarrassing questions. I
liked her.

A siren sliced the air just as I was getting into Boyd's
car to move it to the taxi lot. The high-pitched whine
was nearing when I started the car and leisurely drove it
around to an alley that three blocks later brought me up
behind the taxi building. I pulled the Mustang around
into the space I'd leased, parked and locked the car, and
started walking back to the rental Ford. By the time I was

passing the building where Boyd had recently lived-and-died, both ambulance and police car were parked zig-zaggedly, half in the street, half up on the sidewalk, and half-ass overall when you consider there were plenty of open spaces in front of Albert Leroy's building. But then, parking sensibly isn't in the spirit of an emergency. As if rushing around was going to do Albert Leroy any good.

Actually, the rushing around was pretty well over by now. Two cops were standing with hands on butts as two guys in white were coming down out of the stairwell carrying a stretcher with a sheet-covered Albert Leroy. A few people were milling around, mostly women from the Laundromat down a couple doors, but there was no crowd really, still too early for that. A tall man in his forties, well-dressed, was standing next to one of the policemen, who was asking him questions in a respectful, next-of-kin sort of way. An older man, who'd been standing in the background, moved forward and touched the tall man on the shoulder and seemed to be offering condolences. The tall man nodded his head sadly and the shorter, older man nodded back and turned and walked across the street, in my direction.

As he approached I saw that he wasn't just short, he was very short, maybe five-four, but he carried himself erect and he was a handsome old guy. His features were well-defined and though deep-set in his face, unmarred by age, and the character lines down his cheeks were straight, slashing strokes. He was wearing a white shirt, rolled up at the sleeves, and loose brown trousers and when he passed by me, he muttered, "Poor old soul," as though he expected me to know what he was talking about.

My eyes followed him as he entered Boyd's building, through the front door on street level. As the door closed I noticed the sign in the draped front window: "Samuel E. Richards, Chiropractor."

I stroked my shoulder, said to myself, "Why not?" and followed the old guy inside.

"Sir?" I said.

He turned quickly and smiled. A kind smile, but shrewd. "Yes, young man?"

"You're Dr. Richards?"

"I'd better be," he grinned, "otherwise I'd be breaking the law using his office."

"I could use some help."

"Most people could. Wellsir, I'll tell you, I'm not open for business just yet. The wife's cooking up some break-fast and I'll have to take care of that before I take care of you. How about coming back in thirty minutes, half an hour?"

"I can smell the bacon frying. Smells good."

"We got a little apartment set-up to the back of the office. The wife and me're getting on in the years, couldn't manage an office and house both. And she's got arthritis, don't you know, and the steps in our house weren't doing her any good. You know, you got to compromise some-times, so here I am."

I told him it sounded like a nice arrangement. I looked

around; we were in a waiting room, with several chairs and a stand with some old magazines on it. There was no receptionist. "You don't mind if I wait here, do you?"

"Not at all. What you say was wrong with you?"

"My shoulder. Had an accident an hour or so ago."

"What sort of accident?"

"Slipped on the soap in the shower, would you believe it?"

"Surely would," he said, smiling gently. "You'd be surprised how many accidents take place in bathrooms. Well, you come on in the other room, we'll get you on the table and get you relaxed. Shouldn't take more than five minutes to throw my breakfast down."

His working office was small, just large enough for a desk and chair and two chiro tables, one of which stood upright waiting to be lowered. That was the one he had me climb onto and eased me down and it was comfortable, so comfortable it was hard resisting the urge to sleep.

I turned my head to one side, a painful move considering my shoulder, and studied the room; the walls were a soothing pastel green, recently painted, but everything else was old: the desk and chair were scarred with age and the chiro tables had been in action for some time. On the wall was his diploma, or first license, and it was brown with age. I squinted and read the date: "1921." I was still in that position, looking over the room, when he came back from a very hasty breakfast.

"Get your head back in the slot, there, boy, twisting your neck to the side isn't doing your shoulder any good."

I followed his advice and felt his fingers on my neck. He probed my neck and upper back, said, "Oh yes, here's the problem," and went to work.

He was good. Very. A pro. His fingertips were super-sensitive and his moves were powerful but painless. He had a knack for catching me off guard. He'd say something conversational, like, "Going to be a rainy one," and as I'd start to reply, down he'd come, like a man twice his size and half his age. "That was my Sunday punch," he'd laugh softly, and go on to something else. He gave me fifteen minutes of adjusting, most of it spent on my shoulder, but some of it on my neck and lower back, and when he lifted the table up and I got off, I felt fine. I told him so.

"Glad to hear it," he said. "That's my real satisfaction, getting quick results. Good idea getting here soon after you took your fall, too. Easy working on something like that right after she happens. Couple days go by and all kinds of tension sets in."

"You don't use X-ray?" I asked him, remembering bills I'd paid to a chiro in Wisconsin.

He held up his hands, flexing his fingers. "These is X-ray enough."

I nodded, said, "Listen, how old are you, anyway?"

"Eighty-one, this January past."

"That's remarkable."

"Maybe so, I don't know. I'm not so good as I was once, but I guess I'm still good enough. When I get past a certain point, I'll give it up."

"Oh?"

"You got to be sure you get results, every time. Otherwise you should give up what you're doing. Do it right or not at all."

"You get results, take my word. How much I owe you, anyway?"

"Four bucks," he said, and I gave it to him. He explained in detail how all the other chiros in town had gone up to six, but he couldn't see charging that much. He was one of those talkative old guys who enjoy having someone to do their talking at. I wondered if maybe I couldn't work that to my advantage.

"Say," I said, "what was all that commotion across the way?"

He shook his head. He sat at the chair at the desk and I sat on the table next to it. He said, "Terrible thing, terrible thing, that. Poor old Albert Leroy. Poor old boy. Old, I say... I'm eighty some and he was, what, maybe forty, but he was older than me. Much. He didn't have a soul. No wife, wasn't particular close to his relatives. Didn't have a profession to speak of. No goals, no pride in anything."

"What happened to him, anyway?" I had him going good now, all I had to do was prod him gently now and then. What a find.

"Somebody shot him, appears. Appears he was robbed." He shook his head some more. "Doesn't surprise me, people getting the wrong idea about old Albert. Figuring he had money stashed in his place somewheres. I'll bet dollars to doughnuts he didn't have a penny hid. So somebody shot him and for nothing, I'll wager."

He was right about that. I said, "Why would anyone think this fella had money?"

"Well, his family's got money. You from around here?"

"No. I'm a salesman, passing through."

"Still, you might've heard the Kitchen Korner program. They sell the Kitchen Korner products all over the Midwest."

"No, don't think I have."

"There's this radio program, don't you see, called Kitchen Korner, and it's out of Port City but they syndicate it all over this part of the country. It's nothing fancy, just some women sit around and gabble. Recipes, folksy talk and the like. It was started up years ago by an old gal name of Martha Leroy."

"Leroy?"

"The same. Albert's momma. The program usually consisted of old Martha and one of three or four aunts what live in the area, and her little girl, Linda Sue. Wellsir, Martha passed on ten years ago, and her husband, old Clarence Leroy, followed right on her heels. Martha was the pants and Clarence, who had a pretty fair business head, got to feeling his oats with the boss dead and buried, and took up with some filly and died of a heart attack within the month. But that's beside the point. The program, the Kitchen Korner program—that's 'corner' with a 'K,' don't you know—got carried on by the daughter, Linda Sue."

"They make a lot of money with the radio show?"

"Piles, and more off the products. They got a line of

foodstuffs, called likewise Kitchen Korner. Jam and soup, mostly, some other things."

"All of it made in Port City?"

"They make the jam here. The soup, too. They sell all other sorts of business that's made elsewhere, farmed out to manufacturers who ship the stuff here, where it gets a Kitchen Korner label pasted on. Old Martha's on the label, smiling from eternity. The old gal's immortal, if you call sitting cold as can be in a thousand refrigerators immortal."

"Why wasn't this Albert in on the money?"

"Wellsir, Albert was a funny one. Always kind of quiet-spoken. Stayed to himself as a kid. One of my sons went to school with him and said the other kids used to pick on Albert and make fun of him, 'cause he was something of an odd-looking duck." Again, he shook his head. "And kids can be cruel. Real cruel. Near as cruel as adults."

"Yes."

"Anyway, he was pretty good in the brains department, Albert was. High I.Q. and all. High school salutatorian. But when he went off to college, well, he had problems… some folks said it was a girl he got stuck on who played him foolish…others say he couldn't get along without his momma at his side, he always was sort of sheltered by old Martha. However the reason, he come back from his mental treatment even stranger than before, different…" He whispered this, as though Albert might be listening in. "…sort of a vegetable, don't you know. Not bright like before, nosir. Mumbling, stuttering, shuffling…it was a sad sight, I mean to tell you."

"Has he been an embarrassment to his family?"

"I hope to shout. But Albert never caused 'em any harm. He went his own way. He's always been a friendly sort, in his quiet manner, and most people speak kindly of him, if they speak of him at all. Matter of fact, I always thought it was kind of low of that family, the way they didn't look after Albert."

"Oh?"

"His momma wasn't near so partial to him after his breakdown, and his poppa never paid him much mind to begin with. After the mother and father died, Linda Sue… which seems to me kind of a silly name for her, now that she's a woman of forty-five…Linda Sue told Albert to move out of the house. The Leroy home is one of those mansion-type things up on the West Hill, looking out on the river, don't you see, one of those real old beauties up there, know the ones I mean?"

"Yes."

"They gave him a janitor job down in South End where they make the soup, but that's all they done for him, far as I know. Some folks think Albert had money left to him, others think his janitor pay was high, like as if he was an executive, but was storing it away, hoarding, like a hermit. I suppose that's what led to what happened to him. Somebody took a gun up there and shot him and went searching for buried treasure." He laughed. "Dollars to doughnuts whoever-it-was didn't find a thing."

"You were talking to somebody across the street, a tall man. Who was that?"

"Raymond Springborn. Linda Sue's husband. His family has money, too, got a lot of land holdings and property round town." He leaned over, confidentially. "Some folks don't know it, but I hear he's part owner of that nightclub place, the one run by that girl who did that nudie thing in that Bunny book. Ah, that's the name of the place, Bunny's. He's in it with that gal, and isn't that pretty company for the hometown Kitchen Korner boy." He cleared his throat. "Not to be disrespectful. I'm sure he isn't having anything but business dealings with that gal. Mr. Springborn's okay. Got a hell of a fine business head."

"Sounds like you know him pretty well."

"I sure do. He's my landlord, don't you know. Why you're sitting in one of his buildings right now. If you look out front you'll see it carved in the stone: Springborn Apartments."

20

Cyprus was in the valley between East and West Hill and was a street which seemed to slash the town in half. Located on Cyprus was the local newspaper's office, the county hospital, a public high school, a Catholic grade school, half a dozen churches and, just before the street turned into Highway 22, a drive-in movie playing a couple of skin flicks. I didn't care about any of that. I was on Cyprus not for a guided tour of Port City, but because I was looking for Fuller Street.

Fuller was an offshoot of Cyprus and ran up the edge of West Hill, just as West Third Street ran up the outer edge of the Hill, on the riverfront side of town. Fuller cut through a respectable middle-class residential area, mostly two-story white clapboards that had seen better days but were far from rundown, while West Third crossed through the section filled with near-mansions that were old but not visibly decaying. Raymond Springborn and his wife Linda Sue lived in one of those near-mansions on West Third. Peg Baker lived in an apartment house just off Cyprus on Fuller, in the dip before the rise of the Hill. Between them was Port City.

The apartment house was two-story red brick trimmed in white, white wrought-iron handrails along the upper

floor winding down around a wide cement stairway that
came up the center front of the building. The structure
had a blandly ageless quality: it could've been put up
twenty years ago or yesterday. The parking lot was bigger
than the ten-apartment complex required, and looked as
though it might've been installed by a landlord who dis-
liked mowing lawns; there were little squares of grass and
shrubbery stuck here and there around the concrete
lawn, like sprigs of parsley on a big empty plate.

I pulled the rental Ford into the largely vacant lot,
only a third-filled now as it was past nine and folks were
off to work, these cars remaining being second cars, or
belonging to people who worked nights, like Peg Baker. I
snuggled in between a station wagon and a Volks and
turned off the engine and got out.

The phone book had listed Peg Baker's address as 121
Fuller, and this was 121 Fuller, all ten apartments of it.
Some of the tenants had their names on their mailboxes,
six of the ten did anyway, but not Peg Baker. Knowing six
of the places weren't hers narrowed the field, but not
enough. And the curtains on those four remaining apartments were all closed, too, in case I wanted to risk getting
busted for window-peeking. I could always check with
the manager to see which apartment was Peg Baker's, but
the manager lived elsewhere. On the door of a laundry
room was a notice giving the manager's name and address
and hours at which to call. The hours were in the evening,
but I used the pay phone in the laundry room anyway and
tried the manager's number and a recorded voice asked

me to leave a message after the tone and I hung up. Damn.

I was just getting ready to pick one of the four doors at random and knock when I spotted what had to be Peg Baker's car. Her registration would probably be visible, and on that would be her address. Hopefully that address would be more specific than "121 Fuller."

It was no chore figuring the car as hers. The surprise was I hadn't spotted it immediately, but I hadn't, because it was hidden down there in the end stall on the opposite side of the lot from where I'd parked. It was crouching there behind a big blue four-year-old Caddy.

It was a pink Mustang.

Several years old, but shiny and pink and dentless like new, a sheltered pink baby that never grew up, a Peter Pan of a car, parked way down on the end where nobody could hurt it. The upholstery was pink. The carpeting was pink. The dashboard was pink. The gearshift knob was pink. I was afraid to look under the hood.

My joy at finding the car subsided at once: her registration was taped inside the front window, staring up at me in the face, the useless "121 Fuller" address thumbing its nose at me. It said, "Margaret Anne Baker," and it said, "State of Iowa Motor Vehicle Licensing Bureau," and "Port City" and sundry other bureaucratic bullshit, but nowhere did it say Apartment Number Such-and-Such.

What now? Back to pick a door and ask? I'd have to be careful how I went about it, as the laundry room and several windows were decorated with signs saying "No Solicitors Allowed," warning that a city ordinance called

for the immediate jailing of anyone practicing that for-
bidden art. I reminded myself not to spit on the sidewalk.

I was one hell of a fine detective.

So I wandered back to my car, head hanging low, to
regroup my thoughts. I'd intended getting at Raymond
Springborn via an indirect route, namely Peg Baker. Just
how I would do that, I didn't know; I would improvise, as
time allowed for nothing but improvisation, and then what
else could I have done but improvise, never having done
this sort of thing before. My only other option would be a
frontal approach with Springborn, and what with the body
of his murdered brother-in-law Albert Leroy just fresh
found, now was a decidedly bad moment to approach
Springborn frontally. I could picture myself dropping in
on the mournful family, perhaps while Springborn was
gathering the sympathies of the Port City Chief of Police.
Such a situation could bring up some embarrassing questions, such as, "Who are you?" or "What are you doing
here?"

I sat in the Ford, slouched down, trying to think. For
two cents I would've gone to sleep. For three cents I
would've never waked up. I kept trying to think, trying. I
couldn't. Maybe Broker was right, maybe I was being an
ass, maybe I should give it up. My initial feeling of indignant rage had dissipated by this time. I felt crumpled,
like an empty paper cup, used, emptied, discarded.

I saw him out of the corner of my eye. Didn't recognize him. At first. But he was familiar. I *made* myself
think. And I knew him.

The drummer.

The drummer in the rock band at Bunny's the other night. And Peg Bunny Herself Baker's latest shack-up, if barroom rumor had it right, and what I'd seen of her cow-eyeing him from the sidelines substantiated that rumor.

He was creeping from out the apartment down on the far left corner of the building, bottom floor, over there on the side where the pink Mustang was parked. He had closed the door gently and was moving slowly away, doing the walking-on-eggs bit, carrying tennis shoes in his left hand, holding them gently by his fingertips. He looked like a guy in a cartoon sneaking in late after a night's drunk, only to be caught and clobbered by a shrew with a rolling pin. Except this guy was sneaking out, not in, and did not fit the henpecked hubby stereotype. His was another stereotype: long blond shaggy shoulder-length hair, stubbly beard, shirtless, faded blue jeans with "LOVE" stitched up the crotch.

I sat there in the car, still slouched, still unseen by this refugee from a panel cartoon. Oh, I thought idiotically, what I'd give for a rolling pin. I watched him near the pink Mustang; he was shooting furtive glances every half-second, moving carefully, the tips of his dirty toes barely touching cement. I didn't know what this boy was up to, but up to something he was.

He opened the door to the Mustang on the driver's side and crawled in. Crawled I say because he got down on the floor, on his back, poking fingers up under the dash. I sat and watched and for just a moment I wondered what the fuck the clown was doing and when the moment was up, I knew: he was hot-wiring the car.

He didn't see me coming. He was on his back still, but his eyes were watching as his hands scurried up under the dash. He had a pocket knife out and open, stripping insulation from wires, and he knew what he was doing but his work was going kind of slow. I knew why. I could smell the liquor and I was standing and he was down there on his back. So he was a drunk sneaking out, if not in, and who but a drunk would steal a pink Mustang, anyway?

I grabbed him by an ankle and pulled him out. He bumped his head several times on several surfaces and by the time he was out onto the cement he was pretty shook up. I said, "Lose your keys?"

He tried to kick me in the face. I didn't let him. I batted his foot away and he tried to slash me with the knife. I didn't let him do that, either. I kicked the knife out of his hand and it skidded across the cement and into some bushes and I stepped on his throat. Not hard, but with a throat you don't have to step hard, really. His eyes were round and terrified, saucers full of fear. He tried to say something, but nothing came out; it's difficult to speak when someone is standing on your throat. So I eased the pressure to hear what he had to say, lifted my foot completely off and he took the opportunity to say, "Mother-bitch-son-of-a-fucker," which was an indication of how drunk he was.

I yanked him by the arm and he hung sort of in space and then I heard her.

"What the hell's going on here?" she was saying. Her voice was high-pitched, shrill at the moment, but of course she was screaming, so that was natural.

"Is this your car?" I said, nodding to the Mustang.

"It most certainly is!"

"What about him? Is he yours too?"

"I know him. What are you doing to him?" She came a little closer and said, "Jesus, what a stink. Christ, is he drunk. He must've guzzled down every ounce of booze in my apartment." She wasn't looking as good as her *Playboy* picture, or as prick-teasing as her appearance the other night at the club, but Peg or Bunny or whatever she called herself was a beauty, a natural one, and with no makeup and with tousled hair and in an old worn-out blue terry cloth robe that covered her neck to knee, tied round the waist and giving only the slightest hint of the body under there, she was a woman you could screw, not a picture you could masturbate over.

I said, "What I'm doing is stopping him from stealing your car."

"What?"

"He was hot-wiring it."

"What the hell are you talking about?"

"He was hot-wiring it, rigging it so the motor would run without the use of the ignition key."

"What the hell for?"

"So he could drive it away, I suppose."

She came over and kicked the guy right along where the word "LOVE" was sewn. He kind of got away from me then, as he wrenched free so he could grab himself and roll into a ball.

"Fucking asshole," she said. "Why didn't he just steal the keys out of my purse?"

"You got me. Maybe he's so drunk he's stupid. Explain why anybody'd pick a pink Mustang to steal in the first place."

She laughed. Not at all shrill. "Explain why anybody'd own one."

"I was going to ask you about that."

"Maybe I'll tell you. What's your name?"

"Quarry," I said. I don't know why I gave her that name. The moment I said it, I wished I hadn't.

"Let him go, Quarry."

"I'm not holding onto him."

"You know what I mean."

I said to the guy, "Okay. You can go."

It took him half a minute to get to his feet. He looked at the girl for a second, then glanced at me, then took off running, in a limping, just-kicked-in-the-balls sort of way. He was up on the corner of Cyprus after a moment. He stopped there and yelled back, "Bitch! Cunt!" and limped quickly out of sight.

"He means you, I guess."

She grinned. "Well, actually my name's Peg. Peg Baker. Come on in and have a cup of coffee."

"I don't know."

"What don't you know?"

"I don't know if it's safe to hang out with somebody who drives a pink car and sleeps with something like that."

"He slept on the couch. That's where I made him sleep after he couldn't get it up. You want coffee or don't you?"

21

I studied her face and wondered how it could look so hard and so young at the same time and she said, "How about a grapefruit?"

I said, "What?"

"A grapefruit. How about a grapefruit."

She was standing there in the kitchenette, her robe loose enough toward the top for me to get a look at the start of the swell of those Bunny breasts. I sipped my coffee and wondered whether her sexual allusion had been intentional and said, "Yes, I'd like a grapefruit."

"Maybe it's a little late for breakfast-type stuff, what the hell time is it, anyway?"

There was a clock above the window over the kitchen sink but it wasn't running. I checked my watch. "Quarter till ten," I said.

"I suppose you already had breakfast."

"No, I just got up a little while ago myself." I sat at the table sipping the coffee and watched her as she went to the refrigerator and got out a big yellow softball of a grapefruit and sliced it in half on the counter with a long shiny knife. She sectioned the grapefruit halves and lightly sugared them, served them up in bowls and brought them over. She put one in front of me, leaning over so that I got a good look at what was happening under the robe. I took a bite of grapefruit.

"You keep eating," she said. "I'll be right back." She walked from the kitchenette to a cubbyhole hall and went in a door and closed it after her. I turned to the grapefruit and continued eating, slowly, looking around the room as I did.

The room was horrifying. It made no sense that this supposed sexpot from the pages of *Playboy* lived here. This was an old woman's apartment, loaded with memorabilia of decades past. Against the lefthand wall were two oak cabinets that nearly touched the pebbled plaster ceiling, the cabinets crammed full with china and cut glassware. Against the opposite wall was a sofa with doily-pinned arms, as were the arms of the several lounge chairs in the room, and over the sofa was a big mirror with a wooden frame painted gold and carved with cupids and flowers, the mirror reflecting the china cabinets back at themselves. The stucco walls were hung with plates picturing churches and dead presidents. Only the television seemed of this era, a new RCA Color job, but above it, in the corner it took up, was a knickknack rack whose shelves were filled with a salt and pepper shaker collection consisting mostly of little animals and miniature fruit, such as a white and a black lamb, and a pair of plump porcelain strawberries. The front two-thirds of the long room was living room and filled with this chamber of elderly horrors, and the back third was kitchenette. Two waist-high bookcases, with space between to walk through,

divided the room. The books in the cases were not the
sort you might expect from the girl behind Bunny's; they
ran to *Reader's Digest Condensed Books*, a *Collier's Ency-
clopedia*, occasional hardcovers, the raciest of which was
Forever Amber, and scattered romance paperbacks. The
kitchenette seemed largely spared of the senior-citizen
school of interior decorating, outside of the clock above
the sink which was a Felix the Cat clock with jeweled
eyes and a tick-tocking tail, which was silenced now because the plug was pulled. Also, atop the refrigerator was
a cute stuffed toy: a furry pink and black spider about the
size of a healthy rat.

She came back wearing the blue sweater I'd seen her
in a few nights before at Bunny's, though now she was
also wearing matching blue hotpants. Her legs were pale
white and slender but shapely and looked delicious, and
her breasts bobbed up and down as she moved toward
the table, where she sat and began eating her grapefruit,
taking small but greedy little bites, as though she got a
sensuous enjoyment out of every nibble.

"Nice place you have here," I said.

"Pretty fucking grim, isn't it?" she said.

"Looking around I get the feeling you're older than
you look. Who are you, anyway, some hundred-year-old
hag who discovered a fountain of youth?"

"Not exactly. My mother lived here with me, up until
last month."

"What happened last month?"

"She died."

"Oh."

"Aren't you going to say 'I'm sorry to hear that'?"

"I'm sorry to hear that."

"The hell you are."

"Terrible of me to behave so coldly, when your mother and I were such close friends."

She laughed. "I think I'm going to like you…what was your name? Quarry, is that it, Quarry?"

"That's right."

"You got a first name?"

"Do I have to?"

"Sure."

"Make you a deal."

"What kind of deal?"

"You don't ask me my first name and I don't call you Bunny."

"Deal."

"You don't seem overly upset about your mother's death."

"I'm over it. Anyway, it was a blessing, she was senile as hell. I mean, look at this place, that ought to tell you where her mind was."

"Why don't you move all this stuff out?"

"Where to?"

"You got money. Rent some place and store it."

"Oh, I got money, do I?"

"Sure. You own a restaurant or a bar or whatever you call it, you must have money."

"I call it a club and I own half of it. I'm working on owning it all."

"Oh?"

"All or none of it. See, when we started the place we had no idea it was going to go like it did. Business started out big and got bigger. But the business arrangement I got isn't the best."

"Why's that?"

"Well, when I got this idea for a club, I had some money, but not a whole hell of a lot. My mother was getting bed-ridden and like I said, sort of senile, and the big house we had on the hill we sold…"

"You had one of those houses on the hill?"

"Yeah, ours is a Port City family that goes way back. My old man was in the pearl button business, which used to be Port City's claim to fame…Pearl Button Capital of the World! Until plastic came along and the pearl button market fizzled. Dad sold out early, and we had enough money to maintain the house on the hill and he and mother lived comfortably until Dad died five, six years ago and Mother started needing medical attention."

"Didn't I see all this on a soap opera?"

"Oh eat shit, Quarry. Anyway, I sold the house, moved Mother and all her possessions into this cozy two-bed-room flat and put up a chunk of money for the place you know as Bunny's. I also provided the concept of the place and my shady reputation as the Port City fallen lady who was nude in front of God and everybody, and my business partner provided the land and the rest of the money. Because his investment, as far as land and capital is concerned, was bigger than mine, his share of the profits is bigger. I want more of the money than I been getting. More, hell, I want it all. I'm the fucking Bunny! If he wants the money, let *him* pose bare-ass."

"You're going to try to buy him out, then?"

"Yeah, I been saving my share of the profits like a good little miser. And if I can't buy him out, I'll make him buy me out and I'll build another club someplace."

"Listen, I want to ask you something."

"Go ahead."

"The pink Mustang. Where'd you get it?"

"It was a present. Back in my Bunny days. Maybe if I get to know you better I'll tell you about it."

"I'd like to know you better."

"I know you would."

"Is that right?"

"That's right. This morning was no accident, was it?"

I choked on my bite of grapefruit. "...pardon?"

"This morning. You came around here looking for a way to get close to me, didn't you? Don't play dumb. I saw you a couple nights ago, at the club. I saw you staring at me."

I grinned, more in relief than anything else. "I'm sorry. Couldn't help staring."

"A lot of men stare at me. Most of them stare at me like I'm so much meat, Grade-A U.S. government-inspected prime maybe, but meat just the same. You, you stared at me like you were staring at a woman."

"You can really tell the difference, huh?"

"Sure can. I get that goddamn meat stare all the time.

Almost every son of a bitch in Port City's tried to get in my pants one time or another."

"But you're selective."

"That's right."

"Then let me ask you something."

"Go ahead."

"You won't get mad?"

"Ask and see."

"If you're selective, what are you doing shacking with a freak like that one who tried to heist your wheels?"

She laughed. Her eyes laughed too, sparkled sort of. "I got a weakness for younger men. How old are you, anyway?"

"How old are you?"

"I'm thirty-two."

"I'm younger."

She smiled. She touched my hand. "Thanks for stopping that creep. I like that car of mine, I'm fond of it, it's got sentimental meaning for me."

"He was drunk."

"Yeah, well, he sat around smoking pot last night and then he couldn't get straight and I kicked him out of the bedroom, locked the sucker out, in fact. He must've sat up all night drinking up my liquor stock and planning his revenge."

"I didn't think he knew what he was doing."

"Maybe he did. That was his band's last night at the club, you know, and he told me the group was going to have to break up pretty soon, 'cause him and another guy had the drug rap hanging over 'em and the two of 'em were planning to hotfoot it to Canada. Maybe he got inspired and was going to drive my Mustang over the border."

"Or maybe he's gay and pink just appeals to him."

"He just might've been, at that. Most men react pretty favorably to me, that's the first time I can remember any guy having trouble."

"Younger guys, huh?"

"Yeah. Younger guys, and guys moving through town, one-night stand things, you know? I like short relationships. Short and sweet. A long relationship to me is one that lasts a week."

"Is that so? You steer away from the locals, huh?"

"Goddamn right. I like being on my own. Get involved with somebody around here and before you know it, I'd be into something serious. No true, deep abiding loves for me, thanks, I been stung by that shit before. No meaningful mature relationships with married men, either, I seen too many girls get shafted in the ear by that stuff. I like my relationships nice and shallow. One-night stands, yessir. And then there was my mother. When she was alive I couldn't have men friends in, now could I? So it was motel rooms and backseats of cars and such. Little sordid, maybe, but it serves the purpose. I mean, everybody has to get their rocks off now and then."

"I know what you mean."

"What do you do for a living, anyway?"

"I'm a salesman."

"Then of course you know what I mean. Your goddamn life's a chain of one-night stands, isn't it?"

"Isn't everybody's?"

She stopped for a moment, looked thoughtful, looked at me. "I wonder," she said.

It was silent for a while, and just as the silence was getting to the awkward stage, I said, "This grapefruit is good."

"You want another half?"

"Only if you do."

"I do."

"Okay then."

She got another huge yellow softball and served it up and said, "Florida grapefruit."

"Thought so. Really fine."

"Yeah, girlfriend of mine sent a crate of 'em up to me. Now there's an example of what I was talking about."

"Huh?"

"This girlfriend of mine. She's one who got involved with a guy, a married one at that, and she got shafted in the ear, as well as every other opening on her the son of a bitch could find. That's one of the reasons I'm trying to get out of business with him."

"Wait a minute…you mean the guy this girlfriend of yours was involved with is the same guy you're in business with?"

"Shit, I shouldn't be talking about all this."

"I'm from out of town, Peg, what do I know?"

"Well, see nobody in town knows about the affair between these two."

"You know."

"Yeah, I do, but the guy himself doesn't know I know about it. Whew, confusing, huh?"

"Don't stop now, you got me interested."

"Well...okay. Shouldn't hurt. After all, I'm not using names, am I? And if I did you wouldn't know who I was talking about."

"That's right," I said. Raymond Springborn.

"This guy I'm in partnership with, he's a crackerjack businessman, terrific businessman, really, and fairly ethical as far as that goes, though part of that has to do with his hometown image. Anyway, my best girlfriend was this guy's, what, mistress? Mistress for over a year. He kept her in an apartment and treated her all right, except that the apartment was more like a prison, since he's a fanatic about keeping their affair an utter secret. Then last month he told her their big love was kaput for now, and he sent her down to Florida and he's paying through the nose to keep her down there, and he's leading her on that he's going to start back up with her as soon as he feels things are safe again."

"You think his wife found out or what?"

"Maybe, but that's no big thing. Ray, I mean this guy, and his wife never have been a passionate couple or anything. Separate bedrooms and all that. It's just their business, the family business, has to do with Mom, the Flag and Apple Pie, and shacking up with girls half your age doesn't fit the wholesome American Christian businessman image."

"Interesting."

"Brother, that bastard, he calls her up and says, 'Get out of that apartment,' and she comes crying to me and says she's going to Florida. Brother."

"He kept her in an apartment here in town?"

"Sure. Easy enough for him. He owns apartments all over Port City. He owns this building here, for one, and the building her apartment was in is downtown."

"Downtown. Wasn't that risky, a central location like that?"

"Hell, he was her goddamn landlord. Who's going to talk about a landlord calling on a tenant? Anyway, the building isn't on the main drag downtown, it's off on one of the side street business districts. And nobody else in the building would have ever suspected anything going on. Ray, the guy I mean, keeps the middle apartment empty, and she was on the top floor, with some old people on the bottom."

"Old people?"

"Yeah, some old guy has the bottom-floor business office, with an apartment in back for him and his wife. He's some kind of doctor or something. A chiropractor, I think."

22

She parted her legs and I crawled up on top of her and slid easily inside. We took our time, as we'd had no foreplay, but she was slick and wet and no trouble getting into and we moved together, instinctively together, working slowly, silently, to a gushing mutual peak where the first sounds from either were simultaneous, semiverbal sighs.

I stayed on top of her for a minute or so, one hand still under her ass, cupping one cheek, the other hand cupping a full breast, the nipple of it going from a hard point to a gentle nudge against my palm. I nuzzled her neck and she rolled her head slowly around, liking it. I felt myself getting small, sliding out of her by nature not by choice, and she eased out from under me and off the bed and padded out of the bedroom into the bathroom, her ass jiggling beautifully as she went.

I flipped over on my back, reached over to the nightstand and yanked a tissue from the Kleenex box and wiped myself off. My stomach muscles were aching, but pleasantly; I felt drained, but in a nice way. And my shoulder wasn't bothering me at all. I propped a pillow up behind me, half-sitting, half-lying, and stared at the ceiling.

Earlier, when we'd finished the second grapefruit, we had moved into the living room, continuing our small talk. But as we approached the sofa, Peg had said, "This place is too goddamn depressing, it's like talking in a rest home," and I'd followed her into the bedroom, where her unmade double bed had obviously been slept in on one side only. The room wasn't much different from the rest of the apartment; the furniture in here was just as pedestrian as out there, though unlittered by doilies and knick-knacks. Just another study in stucco-walled apartment complex typicality, though considerably livened up by a smattering of posters, the brightest being reprints of gaudy old film ads from the Thirties, one showing King Kong having a gay old time atop the Empire State Building, another showing the Marx Brothers having equally good a time at the circus. There was also an orange poster showing an underground cartoonist's vision of pinheaded men with very thick legs and large feet dancing in a line, the words "Keep on Truckin'" over their heads. Next to that was a poster of that pointy-eared spaceman from TV, while on another two rhinos humped below the words "Make Love Not War." The most striking was a black-and-white poster of Marilyn Monroe's face, right over the bed. The effect of them was strange, as instead of counteracting the elderly aura of the outer apartment, these posters, these free spirits, seemed imprisoned in this room in this old folks home of an apartment, and seemed to be looking at me, saying, "What are we doing here?" I couldn't help but wonder if Peg had put them up to keep sanity while her mother was alive and dominating this world, or if she had put them up since her mother's death, for company. I didn't ask and she didn't tell me. All she did was sit down on the bed, right under the Monroe picture, and look at me with her lips slightly parted, as though she were going to say something, going to actually continue the small-talk we'd begun over grapefruit. But she hadn't done that. I'd put a finger to her lips and had pulled the blue sweater gently over her head. She hadn't protested. In fact she'd gone on to slip out of her hotpants and the blue lacy panties and helped me out of my clothes.

I heard water running in the other room and I sat up straight and called out, "What are you doing?"

"Taking a bath! Care to join me?"

I walked into the bathroom. She wasn't in the tub yet; she was leaning down testing the water. I touched her back and she turned around and came into my arms and we kissed. It was a long kiss.

She said, "That's the first time you ever kissed me."

"I've only known you an hour and a half. Give me a chance."

"Well, you screwed me. I'd think you would've had the decency to kiss me before you screwed me."

"You didn't seem to be interested in kissing."

"I guess we both sort of skipped the preliminaries."

"I guess so."

"I guess people don't kiss as much as they used to."

"I guess not."

"I guess they'd rather get down to business."

"I guess."

We kissed again. Just as long. "You know something?" she said.

"What?"

"It's too bad kissing's gone so out of style."

"Why's that?"

"It's nice. Next time, tell you what."

"What?"

"Let's not skip the preliminaries."

"You complaining about my technique?"

"Hardly."

We kissed again. Shorter this time.

"Let's get in the tub," she said.

"Okay," I said.

We got in, her in front; I soaped her back and kissed her neck.

She said, "I always take a bath after I screw."

"Always?"

"Always."

"What if you screw in the backseat of a car?"

"I sponge-bathe," she said, and laughed. "No, you silly bastard, I take a bath as soon as I get home, in that case."

"You like baths."

"Yeah. You suppose I take baths after I screw because of guilt feelings? Like Lady Macbeth washing the blood off her hands?"

"I don't know. I like to swim."

"That's like bathing."

"Only you don't have to fuck around washing."

"Why do you suppose you like to swim, Quarry?"

"I like the feeling of water on me. All over me."

"Pass the soap up here."

"Okay."

"Quarry."

"Yeah?"

"You want to hear about the pink Mustang?"

"Sure."

"It's kind of personal."

"I just screwed you, didn't I? How much more per-sonal can you get?"

"Screws aren't always personal."

"Oh?"

"Ours was a pretty personal screw. In twenty years I could tell somebody about that screw. How many screws can you remember well enough to tell about them the next day, even?"

"What about the Mustang?"

"There was this guy in Chicago. I was working as a Bunny in the club there, you know? He saw me in the magazine, the nude pose. He fell in love-at-first-sight with me, he said. He kept coming around the club, both-ering me. It was getting me in trouble, almost lost me my job, you're not supposed to fraternize with the customers, you know. So I agreed to go out with him, if he wouldn't pester me. I went out with him and I didn't like him at first. He wasn't crude or anything, not your preconceived notion of what a gangster would be...oh, I didn't mention that, did I? He was a mob person of some kind. I suppose he killed people, or had them killed, but I didn't think about that. If I'd've known for sure, it might've bothered me, so I never asked. We went together for a year and six months. He took me all over, Las Vegas, the Bahamas once. Then I found out he had a wife. I was humiliated. Oh, I wasn't that much of a Iowa hick, I'd dated married men before, but I'd always known. I was with him a year and six months and he never told me, never mentioned it. He was older than he looked, he was fifty maybe and looked forty, and he was married to some old broad who didn't care if he studded around. When I got upset, upset about his being married, he bought me a present. See, *Playboy* picks a Playmate of the Year, you know, and that year they gave the winning Playmate a pink Mustang. So he gave me a pink Mustang. He said I was his Playmate of the Year, and I guess I should have been insulted by the implication of that, but I knew how he meant it and it made me cry. He gave me the pink Mustang and told me he'd call me in a week, after I had some time to forgive him. But during that week he died. Or was killed, maybe, I don't know. He was found in his garage, door shut, car running, the carbon monoxide killed him, accidentally, on purpose, whatever. What's it matter? That was seven years ago. I keep the Mustang in top shape. It's like new. It's going to kill me when I have to junk it, eventually."

"Do you remember the first time you screwed with him?"

"No," she said, a hint of surprise in her voice. "No, he couldn't screw for shit."

She didn't say anything for a moment and then I realized she was crying. I wanted to help her but didn't know what to do. I touched her shoulder and that seemed to do the trick.

We were putting our clothes on in the bedroom when I heard something outside that sounded like thunder. I went to the window and drew back the curtain and it was thunder. "I'll be goddamned," I said, "the sky's black. It's going to rain like a son of a bitch."

"My windows are down," she said.

"Mine too." I crawled into my trousers, zipped up and moved out of the room. "I'll go out and take care of it."

I stepped out the door and the sky rumbled again and I ran to the Mustang, rolled up the windows, ran to the Ford, got my raincoat out of the backseat, rolled up the windows. A few drops of rain streaked my face and just as I got to the door the downpour began. Inside, I threw my raincoat down on the hard straightback chair next to the door and heard a clunk. My automatic was in the pocket. I hoped Peg wouldn't run across it.

"Does it shock you," she said, dressed in blue sweater and hotpants again, sitting on the sofa, "that I was a gangster's woman?"

I laughed.

She smiled, but there was a hint of frown in the smile. "What's so damn funny?"

" 'I Was a Gangster's Woman,' " I said. "Sounds like something on the cover of *True Confessions*."

She laughed. "That's me. A real gun moll."

"His business didn't seem to bother you."

"His business was his business. He only supplied what others demanded."

I nodded.

"But," she said, "if I'd known exactly what he did, I probably wouldn't have stood for it."

"That's hypocritical as hell."

"Hey, who appointed you preacher, Quarry? You're awful moral all of a sudden."

"Maybe you've just underestimated me."

"Bullshit. Next thing you're going to tell me is you're not married."

"I'm not."

"Every traveling salesman is married."

"Not this one. You're even my first farmer's daughter."

"Sure. You're my first man, too. Today." She shook her head, smiled crookedly. "You know something?"

"What?"

"Something about you reminds me of Frank."

"Who's Frank?"

"My gangster. My poor dead gangster."

"I thought you said I screw better."

"Oh you do, you do. So far, anyway. But your eyes. There's something in them, or something that isn't in them..."

"Listen, I want to know something. Does it or doesn't it bother you that this Frank was in the rackets?"

"It doesn't bother me. So am I, in a way. You know, that guy I mentioned before? The one I'm in business with? The one who shafted my girlfriend and sent her down to Florida for his health?"

"Yeah. Ray."

"That's right. Ray. How'd you know his name?"

"You let it slip two or three times."

"So I did. Anyway, some of Ray's money comes from that kind of people."

"What kind of people?"

"Mob kind of people."

"You mean he's running businesses as fronts for them?"

"No. All his businesses are legitimate. But he's done a lot of expanding, and some of the mob people in the Quad Cities channel money into his businesses, mainly 'cause it's a good investment. Not to mention the last thing anybody'd suspect as being backed by that kind of money." She touched her forehead. "Hey, that reminds me…I was supposed to go over to the Springborn place this morning. Going to talk with Ray just once more, and if we can't settle those contractural differences of ours between us, I'll get my lawyer to move on it. What time is it, anyway?"

"Quarter after eleven."

"Shit! I was supposed to be over there at eleven!" She got up from the sofa and said, "I better call him and tell him I got, uh…waylaid." She grinned and glided over to the telephone on the wall in the kitchenette. I followed her in and sat at the table and watched her dial.

"Mr. Springborn, please," she said to the phone. She winked at me while she waited for Springborn. Finally she was saying, "Hello Ray, look, I'm sorry I didn't make it over this...huh? What? You're kidding?...Oh my God, that's terrible, that's awful, the poor guy...What was it, robbery?...I can't believe it, I just can't believe it...Well, listen, what we have to talk about can sure wait until... Really?...Well, okay...Two-thirty then."

She hung up, shaking her head, and I said, "What was all that about?"

She told me. She told me about Albert Leroy dying. She explained that Albert Leroy was a simple, harmless guy who was Springborn's brother-in-law, a quiet little man who'd had a nervous breakdown once and afterward was never the same. No one in the family, she told me, gave a damn about old Albert; a lot of folks in town thought it was a sin that the Springborns gave Albert a token janitorial job at the soup plant and let it go at that. It was something of a pain, she said, hearing Ray Springborn pretending to be upset, just as it would be a pain to watch Linda Sue Springborn going through the motions of mourning. She said as an indication of how callous the Springborn reaction to the death was, Ray had told her to come on over for their business chat this afternoon, to help him "take his mind off the tragedy." I asked her how it happened and she said, "Robbery, they say. His place was ransacked. You see, it's almost a legend in town that Albert was something of a pack rat. And the Leroy family has been a money family in Port City for years. Somebody must've figured they'd find a mattress full of money."

"Too bad."

"Yeah. Sure as hell is."

Thunder cracked again. The rain was coming down hard. She went to the window over the sink and parted the curtains and looked out at the rain slanting down and it reflected back on her face, running down her cheeks in gray streams. She said, "You know something, Quarry?"

"What?"

"I wish I hadn't cried this morning."

"What?"

"Because now I haven't got any crying left in me. And it seems to me like somebody ought to shed a tear for that poor son of a bitch Albert Leroy."

23

By early afternoon the rain let up, but the sky was black and constantly spitting, an arrogant reminder that this was only a temporary reprieve. The hot summer rain had taken the air away and left in its place a humid cloud, a dank overcast through which the Springborn place looked unreal, like something off the cover of a gothic paperback. But it was the mood of the afternoon that was gothic, not the house, which was a massive but fairly commonplace two-story structure, red brick trimmed with white-painted wood, the brick faded and smoothed by age to the color of rust. Outside of a rococo effect from the curlicued wood trim, the only vestige of nineteenth-century pretension was the single central box tower that sat on top of the two-story building like a little separate house that'd been plopped down on the big one. This was a house built by common folk who'd made it rich, an ordinary brick house only slightly puffed up by wealth.

There could be little doubt, however, that this was an important home: in a neighborhood crowded with would-be palaces, only the Springborn place had half a block to itself, sitting far back on a gentle hill of a lawn, graveled private drives on either side. The drive on the right led to a red-brick four-door garage large enough to barrack a hippie commune, and at present both drives were jammed with cars, as though the big old home were a way-station hotel filled with guests stranded during a storm.

We parked in front, or so I thought; when I got out of the Ford and stood and got a good look I could see we were facing the ass-end of the house. Somehow I resented that, it seemed vaguely pompous to me, even though it made sense to take advantage of the river view. But it was sort of hypocritical for this "common man's mansion" to turn its back on a public street.

We stood at the big solid oak front door (or back door, depending on how you look at it) and Peg said, "Thanks for coming with me."

"I'm going to feel like a fool," I said. "A stranger coming around at a time like this."

"You're not a fool and you're not a stranger, you're my escort and shut up about it."

I was glad to shut up about it. Peg's asking me along had saved me from having to fish for an invitation from her. So far I'd managed to pump her for a lot of information without making myself seem overly curious, and now I was getting inside the Springborn house, again without causing any suspicion on Peg's part or hopefully on anyone else's. What better way to get inside the Springborn place than to come with a friend of the family, with the rest of Albert Leroy's mourners. It beat hell out of breaking-and-entering.

My knock was answered by an attractive woman in her mid-forties. She was slender, her graying black hair pulled back in a neat bun; she wore a flowing but conservative black dress which came down to her knees in a straight and waistless line. Her face was smooth, the skin pulled almost tight, while her neck was heavily creped, indicating a probable face-lift. Her features were intelligent and well-formed, her eyes widespread and alert. She smiled at Peg and nodded, an artificial smile with pain in it, or the semblance of pain, as though she wanted to make sure we knew that she was distraught but in control.

"Thank you for coming," she said, her voice a steady contralto, and she reached for Peg's hand, squeezed it and gave it back.

Peg said, "I'm so sorry about all this, Linda Sue. This must be a horrible time for you and Ray."

She nodded gravely, then looked at me and arched an eyebrow. "I'm somewhat confused today, in the aftermath of this tragedy...I must admit I can't seem to recall your friend, Peg...you'll have to excuse my rudeness..."

"This is Mr. Quarry. He's not a native of Port City, but he's a close friend of mine and was with me when I got the news about Albert. I didn't think you'd mind if he accompanied me."

"Of course not," she said. "I only wish we'd been able to meet under more pleasant circumstances, Mr. Quarry. Won't the two of you come in, please."

We stepped inside and were standing in a hallway that could have been a ballroom, what with its empty impressive size, or perhaps a chapel for some strict Protestant sect, what with all its austere dark wood. The most striking thing in the otherwise vacant hallway was a deep polished wood stairway that curved down from a darkened second floor.

"May I take your coat, Mr. Quarry?"

I gave her the raincoat, having since removed the nine-millimeter automatic and left it in the trunk of the Ford. I felt somewhat naked in this house without the gun, not knowing precisely what kind of confrontations I might be having in here, but it seemed less than wise to tote around the murder weapon of Albert Leroy in the home of his mourning relatives. My uneasiness was amplified by the draftiness of the hallway; it was cool in here, centrally air-conditioned I supposed, an uncomfortable, morgue-like coolness.

Linda Sue Springborn said, "Will you join us in the drawing room, Mr. Quarry?" She motioned to a doorless archway to her left. "Raymond's in the den waiting for you, Peg." She smiled and said, "I understand you're going to discuss business matters. I'm glad you are, that will make things easier for Raymond, get his mind off this very depressing day."

Peg nodded, smiled at Mrs. Springborn, smiled apologetically at me, pressed my hand, and disappeared through the French doors opposite the archway.

I followed Mrs. Springborn into the drawing room. She said, "Make yourself at home," and left me to fend for myself. I found a chair in the corner and sat. I was sitting before I realized I was the only person doing so. The other twenty-some people in the room were standing around, trying to look mournful, none of them taking advantage of the chairs and several davenports. I looked around the room and understood.

It was a nice room to visit but you wouldn't want to live there. It was one of those rooms full of chairs you don't sit in, tables you don't set things down on or pick things up off, with bookcases full of leather-bound volumes you don't read, and a fireplace you don't burn wood in and a grand piano you don't play. The walls in here, though, were not the cheerless dark wood of the hallway but a rather pleasant pastel green satin-paper; this was offset by deadly dull paintings stuck here and there, full of meadows where horses postured stiffly and trees seemed made of green and brown plaster.

Mrs. Springborn circulated, like a hostess at a reception, and periodically remembered the occasion, alternating a sad sideways shake of her head with an up-and-down nod, both of which I took to represent her restrained sorrow. No one spoke above a whisper unless they were speaking with Mrs. Springborn and never once did I hear Albert Leroy's name mentioned. I had the distinct feeling Albert Leroy could have walked into the room unnoticed. I had the odd notion that I was the only person in the room who had really known Albert Leroy, the only person who had played any meaningful part in his life, the only one who viewed Albert's death with at least some importance.

This went on for an hour. Sometimes, the room had so little motion the whole thing could've been a painting, and as dull and lethargic a painting as the landscapes on the walls. I was getting thirsty, in spite of the coolness of the room, and must've swallowed several times, in a dry sort of way, because Linda Sue Springborn came over after a while and stage-whispered, "Could you use a drink of water?" And she winked.

Suddenly I liked her better.

I smiled and said, "Yes, I sure could use a drink of water."

I followed her out of the room and through the hallway into a room that was obviously used for living and not display, with a couch in front of a television and a soft lounge chair next to a table strewn with magazines and paperbacks. From there she led me through a smaller drawing room, not as lived in as the previous room but not as much a museum as the other drawing room, either. Off of that was a small overblown closet of a room, a small study with a desk and one wall of books and three walls of awards and photos relating to the Kitchen Korner radio program. "*My* den," she said. "Not near so large as Raymond's, but I need my privacy as much as he does. Maybe more."

She went to the bookcase where in the middle a space was reserved for a cluster of bottles and glasses, which made for a small but sufficient liquor supply. She said, "Sorry, no ice," and poured me a shot of Scotch as though she knew that was what I wanted. It was. She made herself a hasty gin and tonic and had it down before I'd even sipped my Scotch.

"You take that like it's medicine," I said.

"Exactly what it is," she said. "A transfusion for an anemic soul." She smiled. She was rather pretty, in a plastic-surgery sort of way. Her eyes were hazel. "How glad I am for a stranger to talk to. Someone I don't have to play games with."

"Oh?"

"I didn't love my brother, Mr. Quarry. He was a burden in life and he's a burden in death."

"Those words sound cold even to a stranger's ears, Mrs. Springborn."

"Well…" She made a face, and there was sadness in it somewhere. "It isn't true to say I didn't love my brother… I used to love him…I loved him before he became irrational…before he became a hermit…he was a bright man once, Mr. Quarry, maybe a genius, near it anyway…but he had a mental breakdown, was given shock treatment, which was maybe a mistake because afterwards…he was a vegetable. Tell me, Mr. Quarry, how do you mourn a potato?" She laughed, then abruptly the laughing turned to choking and her eyes teared. She brushed away the wetness and fixed herself another drink. She could mix a gin and tonic as fast as I've seen one made. She could down them with the best of us, too. "There's something in your face that makes me feel I can be open like this with you, Mr. Quarry. And Peg, she's a good girl, a smart girl. She's a little wild sometimes, but I don't think she'd bring one of her casual shack-ups along with her. She must think well of you to bring you along."

"Can I have another Scotch?"

"Of course, certainly, let me have your glass. Where are you from, Mr. Quarry?"

"Nowhere, really."

"What's your trade?"

"I'm a salesman."

"What do you sell?"

"Myself, mostly. Like everybody else."

"How true, how true that is. We're all prostitutes, Mr. Quarry, in one way or another. We pursue almighty buck, the great American pastime. But what happens when we *get* almighty buck, Mr. Quarry?"

"I've never had that problem."

"Well, I've had it, I have it now. Once you get there, so what? What's the point of it all?"

"That's a question I never ask myself."

"You just play your role and continue on, survival as an end in itself."

"You might say that."

"We have roles we play, Mr. Quarry, and sometimes playing them we forget who we really are." She laughed, then said, "Do you know," her voice slipping into a flat Midwestern nasal twang, "do you know I've made a pile of money being a homey, down-to-earth Ioway gal? Like to hear a recipe for chocolate marshmallow fudge? Some tips on jarring preserves?" She shook her head and began making her third gin and tonic. I touched her arm.

I said, "Listen, it's none of my business, especially since I don't know how much you can hold, but you've got a role to play out there, with your friends and relatives, and a gutful of gin and tonic might not be the best thing for you to be riding on."

She made the drink anyway, and had it down before she answered. "Leeches," she said. "None of those S.O.B.'s, none of 'em cared about Albert when he was alive. Why should they care now?"

"You're important businesspeople in this town," I said. "They come out of respect to you."

"Leeches," she said.

"You want to go back now?"

"Yes."

I walked her back and she was a bit wobbly on the way, but once in the drawing room she straightened and re-sumed her role of stiff-upper-lipped bereaved sister. She was a good actress.

24

After a while I went out into the hallway and sat on the bottom step of the winding staircase. It was nice getting away from that drawing room full of ghouls; it was nice sitting alone. For half an hour I sat and watched the French doors to Springborn's den and waited. Finally Peg came out and gave me a wry smile and said, "Having a good time?"

"Terrific," I said. "Any progress?"

She shook her head no; still a stalemate situation, she told me, probably best sorted out by lawyers. Ray was too good at business wheeling-and-dealing, she said, and she was too stubborn, for either of them to make any headway.

Then she said, "Well, now, look...I suppose I ought to go pay my respects to Linda Sue, and make the rounds talking to the friends and relatives. What a pain in the ass. I suppose you've had your fill of all that? You want to wait out here for me?"

"Sure. Take your time, I don't mind the waiting at all."

"Really?"

"Really."

I watched as she disappeared into the drawing room, then I went in through the French doors.

Raymond Springborn's den was similar to his wife's,

but on a larger scale. One wall was a window that provided a no doubt breathtaking view of the Mississippi, a
view blocked right now by drawn cream-color curtains.
The room was full of dark wood, like the hallway but not
so barren, with a nonfunctional fireplace across from the
French doors, its mantel covered by trophy-style awards,
and much wall space taken up by framed citations, plaques
and photographs pertaining to the Kitchen Korner radio
program and various other Springborn-Leroy family enterprises. The wall opposite the cream-curtained window
was all but engulfed by a desk about the size of a small
tank, a grooved, scarred desk stacked high with paper-
work. The half of the back wall that wasn't taken up by
French doors was a bookcase and in front of the bookcase
was a steel frame cart with a modest supply of liquor and
glasses riding it. Raymond Springborn was standing with
his back to me, replacing a bottle of bourbon on the
stand, getting ready to chug down a healthy glass.

Apparently he hadn't heard me come in, his mind on
the business dealings he'd discussed with Peg, perhaps,
or maybe he was just anticipating the forthcoming jolt of
bourbon.

"I'd like to talk to you, Mr. Springborn," I said.

I startled him. I heard him choke on his swallow of
bourbon and he swiveled, his face intensely surprised and
angered; the moment was close to a comic one, as though
he were a comedian doing a double take. *Was there recognition in that look? Was this the man who earlier today
had tried to take me apart with a wrench?*

"Who the hell are you?" His voice was an even baritone. He'd been edgy there at first, but he calmed down fast.

I couldn't be sure if this was the man with the wrench, couldn't be sure at all: the struggle had been in near-dark, I'd been caught off guard and had been concerned with survival, not with remembering a detailed observation for later. A black T-shirt and a wrench, that was all I could clearly remember about my assailant. Springborn was wearing black, all right, a conservative gray-black suit, out of respect for the deceased, I assumed. That morning when Albert's body was being hauled away, I'd seen Springborn from across the street and had pegged him as tall, but not this tall, not damn near six-four. And I couldn't remember that man with the wrench as being so tall. But then I hadn't stopped to weigh and measure him, either.

I said, "My name's Quarry."

If he recognized the name, he didn't show it. If he *was* the man who'd hired me, and if the Broker had called him today to tell him about my staying around Port City, then Springborn *might* have gotten my name from Broker. At any rate, what he would have gotten for *sure* from Broker was a description, a good detailed description like the one I wished I had of the man with the wrench.

As for Springborn's description, well, he looked like what he was: a successful businessman, the proper lean, hard look of a man who got to the top and stayed there. His hair was the color of ashes, his eyes a similar gray.

Otherwise his features were bland, ordinary. But those eyes, with shaggy, hawkish eyebrows, those translucent gray eyes seemed to take everything in, let nothing out.

"Have we met?" He finished his bourbon in one gulp, put the glass down on the cart top.

"Maybe. That's something I want to find out."

"Do you have any particular reason for talking in circles?"

"I didn't come to answer questions," I said, "I came to ask."

"Now look, I don't know who you are, or who you imagine yourself to be, Mr. whatever-the-hell-you-said-your-name-was, but…"

"Quarry."

"…but I suggest you and your goddamn overbearing manner leave immediately."

"I suggest we talk."

"You're a madman," he said, teetering between irritation and amusement.

"I'm a businessman. Like yourself."

"We've had business in the past?"

"That's something else I intend to find out."

"People who talk in riddles annoy hell out of me."

"People who act like riddles annoy hell out of me."

"Your nerve is amazing, I'll say that for you. Just how did you manage to get in here, anyway?"

"I came with Peg Baker."

"Peg…?"

"You can forget trying to blame her for me. She's just a

little indiscriminate about who she sleeps with, that's all."

"Oh, so you picked her up, got into her confidence and her pants, not necessarily in that order, and used her to get inside my house."

"Something like that."

"You must manipulate people well."

"As a successful businessman you should know all about that."

"I do. I know all the subtleties of the art. But with you I'll dispense with subtlety. With you I'll be blunt. Leave, Mr. Quarry. Leave my house. Now."

"We have business."

"I have an office for such matters. This is my home, and my brother-in-law died this morning and this is no time for business."

"Even when your brother-in-law's death is the business I want to discuss?"

"What?"

"My business involves his death. His murder."

"In that case, you won't mind if I walk over to the desk, pick up the phone and get my good friend Chief of Police Kurriger over here and you can share your business with him. If you *do* mind, I again must suggest you leave my house."

"Go ahead and call. Your good friend Chief Kurriger might be interested in hearing about some of the things I know. A lot of people might be interested in hearing about some of the things I know. Your wife, for instance."

Springborn calmly refilled his glass of bourbon. He

poured me a glass and I drank it while I watched him drink his. His gray eyes were unfathomable. "Okay," he said, "let's go where we can talk and not be disturbed."

"Okay."

He led me out of the den and up the winding stairway. The second floor was dark, shapeless; it was like walking through a cave. Finally Springborn opened a door and flicked a light switch and started up some narrow stairs and I followed him, coming out onto the upper floor of the house, the little box-tower third floor.

In the middle of the room sat a pool table, massive, ageless, its mahogany wood polished and worn and beautiful, and it was as if this table had been here forever and this room built around it only recently. There was indeed a recent look to the room, its walls covered in commercial brown wood paneling of the sort you might see in a remodeled basement; the modern, characterless paneling surrounded the old table anachronistically, the accouterments of the room as timeless as the table: high-backed, leather-seated chairs; long, yellow-shaded windows with the original woodworking; a tall rack with a dozen cues standing like rifles in a case; and an old map of Port City, as faded as parchment, covering most of one end wall, huge but unimpressive in comparison to the table. Only the white ceiling tile and tubular lighting went along with the paneling; the rest of the room belonged to the table, a relic of days when a man had four and a half by nine feet of room to play a game of pool. The colorful balls were racked and waiting for a game, the expanse of cloth stretching out like a green sea.

Springborn took a cue off the rack, chalked it up. He nodded to me to help myself. I chose one and walked to the table and lifted the wooden frame from around the bright balls, walked down to the other end of the table and fired cue into ball into multicolor triangle, shattering it, scattering balls all over the table, two dropping in, one each in both corner pockets down on the far end. I sank another ball, then missed a tough shot; I was having trouble getting used to the table. It was a good table, it was the mother of tables, but the size was bigger than I had played, and the rails were softer and the nap of the cloth smoother than I was accustomed to.

We didn't play a game, really. We just took turns, shooting till we missed. He would run three or four or five, then miss when the only open shot was too difficult; he played a simple but competent game, a workmanlike game. Our styles were similar; I was workmanlike, too, though I could run the balls longer, up to six or eight. But we were an even match, and a money game would've been close.

Neither of us were pool-hall men. He played with friends, I guessed, up here probably, other businessmen he'd invite over, among whom he was likely considered a top-grade player. I played at home, back at Twin Lakes, at tables in a penny-arcade shop across the street from the beach; I played rotation, mostly, with college kids, most of whom could beat the pants off me.

But it was a way to get acquainted, for Springborn and I, and after half an hour of aimless nonplaying, we knew each other well enough to talk.

I sat down in one of the high-backed chairs, laying the cue across my lap. He continued to shoot, leaning over the table, stroking balls into pockets, stopping now and then to line up a complex shot which he would invariably miss.

He finally sank one of his complex set-ups after several attempts, looked over his shoulder at me and said, "Are you a blackmailer, Mr. Quarry?"

"Not in the conventional sense."

"Then what are you?"

"I think you know. I think there is a very good chance that you know."

He stood up straight, forgot shooting pool for the moment, holding his cue tight in his fist, erect, like somebody carrying the flag in a parade. "Frankly, I don't know what you are...other than a damn fool. I get the feeling you're fishing around for something, that you aren't sure of yourself. You've searched out a confrontation with me and now you aren't quite sure what to do with it." He shook his head side-to-side, his lips drawn back tight over very white teeth. "And frankly, Mr. Quarry, you scare me a little, with your implications, insinuations about my brother-in-law's death...murder, if you will."

"Four thousand dollars," I said.

"...what?"

"For four thousand dollars I'll leave you alone."

He laughed. "I guess you are a damn fool at that. As you've said yourself, Mr. Quarry, I'm a businessman, and I'm not about to buy something without knowing what it is."

"Let me ask you something, then. Why would anyone want to kill Albert Leroy?"

He shrugged, sat on the edge of the table. "The robbery motive is the one I accept, I suppose. The pack rat's buried treasure. No one felt malice against Albert, really. He was a harmless enough guy, most people liked him, he had a smile for everybody, even if it was a simpering kind of a smile. I for one will miss him. We used to play pool up here together, Albert and I. He'd come over Sunday, after church, and we'd all have supper together, my wife and I and Albert and the aunts and uncles and cousins who take part in the radio show and the businesses, our weekly family gathering, a forced, silent charade. But after supper Albert and I would come up here and play eight-ball for a few hours, and I'd let him win one out of every three games or so, and the final game I'd let run close, then purposely sink the eight-ball to let Albert win and go home happy."

I thought back to Boyd's surveillance report on Albert Leroy: the list of activities hadn't included visits here. I said, "He came around every Sunday?"

He nodded. "Up until a month and a half ago, when he and my wife had a falling-out, a little family quarrel... You know, Mr. Quarry, you do manipulate people well, you have a way of sneaking up on a person...you've had me talking when you should have been, because if you don't start talking in a convincing manner about *something* I'm going to toss you out on your ass, and from up here that could be painful."

I said nothing; I was confused.

"Look," he said, "just why are you asking questions about Albert, anyway?"

"Trying to establish a motive."

"A motive for what?"

"His murder. I want to understand why you hired somebody to kill your brother-in-law."

His face reddened and he got slowly to his feet. He raised the cue as if to strike me and said, "I ought to break this thing over your head! You stun me. You crazy son of a bitch, where do you find the incredible, idiotic nerve to come barging into my house, a complete stranger, and blurt out an insane accusation like that!"

"Maybe you'd feel better about it if you were swinging a wrench instead of a cue."

He got a puzzled look on his face; had what I'd said *really* been a non sequitur to him, or was this a mask? He said, "You're insane. Get out of my house."

"Not without four thousand dollars."

He looked at me blank-faced for a moment. Then he started to laugh.

Now I was the startled one.

He said, "I have to give you credit."

I said, "Credit?"

"You're good. Better than you should be. You know, I

ruled Vince out at first, because you didn't look right, you
didn't seem like the type who'd get involved with him.
But this ridiculous attempt to implicate me in Albert's
death…who but Vince could come up with something so
absurd?" He laughed again, more harshly this time. "You
even had me wondering if maybe Peg put you up to this,
to force me into handing Bunny's to her on a platter…
though I couldn't really believe Peg would try anything of
this sort. But Peg is a friend of Carol's and could possibly
have known about Carol and me, so I was thinking about
it."

I swallowed. I wondered what the fuck was going on. I
felt like an actor who had wandered into the last scene of
a strange play.

"Vince is just crook enough," he was saying, "just cretin
enough, to try something ridiculous like this…what's the
matter, isn't he satisfied with the cushy job I set him up
in? Does he know anybody else driving a hack making
that kind of money?"

I didn't know what the hell he was talking about. We'd
been playing a game, both of us, but different games.
Suddenly I was filled with doubt. Suddenly I knew Springborn was *not* the man with the wrench, and that I was
digging a nice deep grave for myself by tossing around all
those hints about Albert Leroy's death.

I stood up and said, "Four thousand isn't so much to
ask."

"No," he said, "it isn't. That's one reason I figure this is
Vince's scheme. A small-time thinker, Vince, a man with

extremely limited vision. Let me give you some advice. You seem like a reasonably intelligent guy. I don't know how in Christ's name you got mixed up with Vince, whether he's a friend of a friend, or somebody you met in service, or someone you ran into in a bar, or what. But however you picked him, you picked a loser, Mr. Quarry. Now. I'd advise you to head back to wherever it is you hail from. Do not pass go. Do not collect four thousand dollars."

"I don't bluff easy," I said, aching to go but for appearance sake not wanting to give in too quickly.

"How much do you know about Vince?"

"Not much," I admitted. Christ, not much.

"You don't…go in for that kind of stuff, do you?"

"What kind of stuff?"

"Maybe you aren't, uh…listen, hasn't he tried anything?" Those gray eyes were trying to tell me something.

"I don't understand you."

"Maybe. Maybe you don't. Well, Mr. Quarry, you just find your own way out. You seem to have enough ingenuity to do that, anyway. I'm going to stay up here and shoot myself some pool…the activities downstairs are too morbid for my tastes. You know, you're not a bad pool player yourself, Mr. Quarry, though you wouldn't do well if we were to play a game for money. When we were shooting around I was sandbagging, you know."

"So was I."

"No you weren't. You were playing full out. It's a naive quality you seem to have. You're a trusting sort, for a blackmailer. However, you do shoot a fair game of pool. But you won't win playing with me. Pool's my game."

"Wrong, Springborn," I said, with some admiration. "Your game is poker."

He bent comfortably over the big old table and batted an eight-ball into a corner pocket and I left him.

25

One thought throbbed through my brain: *get the hell out of here!* I walked quickly across the unlit second-floor hallway, anxious to reach the glowing area of light ahead that marked the top of the winding stairway which would lead me down into that big empty entryway and then outside into dreary, overcast freedom. I'd been an asshole to stay in Port City, an asshole to think I could find my way through so complex a maze in so short a period of time, an asshole to risk everything to regain four thousand dollars and maybe have a shot at avenging Boyd and myself on that son of a bitch with the wrench. Well, I wasn't going to play asshole any longer. I was going to grab Peg by the hand, take her back to her apartment and bang her goodbye, then head on home, to Wisconsin. I actually sighed with relief as I neared the staircase. In the middle of the sigh, somebody touched my shoulder.

I shivered. Not from being cold, though cold I was, cold-sweat variety; I'd been all but running through that hallway like a kid afraid of the dark. And now somebody was touching my shoulder and I didn't know whether to laugh, cry, scream or crap my pants. So I didn't do anything. I waited for something to happen. Linda Sue

Springborn stepped out of the darkness and said, "I heard it all."

She was speaking very softly. This made sense, because she'd just finished eavesdropping and we weren't that far away from the entrance to the tower stairway; we were close enough to hear the distinct clacking together of pool balls in the background.

I didn't say anything. She wasn't acting hysterical. There was no hysteria in that smooth face at all. Had there been, I would've had to loop an arm around her chin and break her neck. A screaming woman was something I could do without right about now.

But she was anything but a screaming woman. She spoke again, her voice soft, very soft, a whisper was a scream compared to this; she said, "Do you want your four thousand dollars?"

It was like a hard blow against the chest, knocking the wind right out of me. But soon I was breathing easily again and I felt a grin tickling the corners of my mouth.

"...you?" I said. "You hired me?"

"Do you want your four thousand dollars?"

I nodded.

"And will you leave Port City?"

I nodded.

"Good. Go downstairs and escort Peg out of the house. She's probably starting to wonder where you are and what you're up to, so don't waste any time. Go ahead, then, and leave with her."

"Leave...?"

"Just walk her out to your car. Then tell her you forgot your raincoat. I'll be waiting in front of the house for you. I'll have your raincoat and the four thousand dollars."

I nodded again.

She said, "Do it quickly. It won't take me more than five minutes to get the money in order. Now go ahead."

"All right."

"Mr. Quarry?"

"Yeah?"

"Why couldn't you just've done it and left town?"

"Good question," I said.

I did as she told me. I went downstairs and found Peg in the drawing room getting her face talked off by a guy in a rumpled suit with a complexion so bad it looked like wax was running down his cheeks. Everybody else in the room was still about as lively as an oil painting, all standing around doing their best to look somber, but this guy was full of smiles and chatter.

"Who the hell was he?" I said, as we walked out of the drawing room into the hall. "He seemed like the only one having a good time."

"Oh sure," Peg said, "he's lotsa yuks. He's the fucking undertaker."

"Well when he goes," I said, "I hope they close the casket."

Peg giggled. "Yeah, that is a nice face he's wearing, isn't it?"

Outside the rain was still holding back pretty much, keeping it down to a light misting. It was getting into late afternoon, but nobody told the sky about it; it was stuck at midnight. On the way to the Ford, Peg told me anecdotes about the various creeps she'd been talking to inside the house, and as I opened the car door for her, I said, "Shit, forgot my raincoat."

"I'll go back and get it for you, Quarry."

"Naw, that's okay. Be back in a flash."

I didn't see Mrs. Springborn at first. She wasn't standing on the porch; she was off to the side, near some shrubbery. She was wearing a long black coat and all that showed up, as I approached, was the whiteness of her oval face, like the face of a madonna, but a madonna with a bad taste in her mouth.

When I reached her, she handed me my raincoat and I put it on. Then she handed me an envelope and let me look inside and count the crisp hundred-dollar bills. There were forty of them. When she saw I was finished counting, she said, "Goodbye, Mr. Quarry."

"Not that easy, Mrs. Springborn."

"Just that easy."

"No. I want to hear about it. I want to know all about why you had your brother killed."

"I'm not going to tell you. My agreement was to pay you. And now here I am paying you again. Which seems payment above and beyond the call of duty, does it not?"

"Are you trying to tell me..."

"That I'm not responsible for your associate's death? Yes. Your...what? Agent? At any rate, the man you work through, the man you know as the Broker, I believe, called me and told me all about your wild story of a man with a wrench. I would imagine it's a true story…you don't seem like a man who'd be prone to hallucination…but, sir, whatever it was that happened to you and your late partner was the result of some unknown factor that neither you nor I had control over, some joker in the deck that neither of us put there."

"If you didn't have my partner killed, and didn't try to have me killed, why pay the four thousand again?"

"To get you the hell out of Port City, why else do you think, you incompetent bastard?" Her low voice sounded almost like a man's—deep, harsh. "Your Broker warned me when he called that there was an outside chance you'd be poking your nose around; he'd take care of it, he said, but there was a slight chance you'd cause some trouble. And then you show up here! I couldn't believe it. Even after we spoke and I knew that you must be who you were, I couldn't believe it! I still don't. My sweet God, I pay close to five thousand dollars for a relatively simple task, a task I could've had performed by some derelict in a bar for fifty dollars, but no, *I* have to have a *professional*, to minimize the risk, to make it safe, quick, someone who'd handle the task with skill…and what do I get? A bumbling fool who kills my brother and then comes to my home making noises about it!"

"All right. I'll leave town. With pleasure. But I want to know. I won't leave until I know it all."

"You ass! You've been incredibly lucky so far…your associate's body hasn't been found yet, for one thing, thanks to this miserable weather you've got me out standing in, and until it's found the police will have no reason to figure Albert's death was anything but a robbery, performed by some idiot who believed the local legend about Albert's treasure. But your friend's body won't go undiscovered forever, and how do you think the police are going to react? We just don't have two murders on one day in Port City, one is a rarity, two is unheard of. Oh, but you aren't afraid of the Port City police, are you? Well there's a man from the Iowa Criminal Bureau of Investigation in this town, and he handles all such matters personally, and he's a professional, Quarry, you do know what a professional is? And how do you think he's going to react when he hears you've been wandering around town asking questions? Take the money, Quarry, and..."

"And run?"

"Yes, damnit!"

"Take five minutes. Take one minute. But tell me."

"No!"

"Then listen to me. I think I know what happened, or part of it."

She was silent.

So I told her.

The way I had it figured, Albert Leroy had found out what was going on between Raymond Springborn and his girlfriend in the apartment across the way. Maybe it had started out as a streak of the voyeur in Albert, maybe he had just come upon the two lovebirds by happy accident, who knew? But come upon them he had, and Albert found power in what he knew, power to come to Raymond Springborn and ask for money, more money than he'd gotten in his job as janitor, that was for sure, probably far beyond that. Maybe he'd asked to be on the goddamn board of directors, or some other sillyass thing he felt he had coming to him as right of birth. Whatever, he had used what he knew to twist Raymond Springborn's arm, and had gotten killed for his trouble.

She remained silent till I was finished. Then she said, "Take the four thousand and go, Quarry."

"I'm close, aren't I?" I said through gritted teeth. "I thought I had it figured *exactly* right, I thought your husband had tried to keep his affair from you, to hide this little girl he was using to scratch his seven-year itch, that he'd hired your brother's death and had done away with the threat of you finding out about his cheating, getting rid of the family deadwood to boot."

She leaned forward and spoke with her lips peeled back, saying, "Do you think I care whether or not Raymond fucks that little whore? Do you think I give a good goddamn if he fucks every bitch-in-heat in the world? I don't want his goddamn bed, I haven't wanted it for years. I *like* the pressure off me!"

"Oh…wait," I said, "wait a minute…no wonder. No wonder. Your husband has never known a thing about this, has he? Damn! Albert came to you with the story about Ray's cheating, didn't he? Albert came to you with the demands."

"This is nonsense."

"It sure is. No wonder your husband was so indignant when I made those implications about him killing Albert! And you, you didn't really give a damn about that little girl he was screwing, did you?"

"I told you, I didn't want to be a part of his damn sex life! Raymond and I, we have an understanding, a way of living together. Our life together is the business. The business is our relationship. We don't have any children, couldn't have any, our family is the business, and our relationship is the business, and why don't you go fuck yourself!"

"You don't want your husband to find out about Albert, do you? You don't want him to know that you had your own brother killed."

"Quarry…"

"And no wonder. A woman who'll murder her brother might do most anything…"

"How much, Quarry? I have another four thousand in the house. Just wait here. I'll get it. I'll get it for you."

"Why did you want him dead? What threat did Albert pose you? You didn't give a damn about your husband's cheating."

She said, quietly, in defeat, "He said…he said he'd tell everyone about Raymond…he'd go to the press and he'd tell them about Raymond and the girl."

And I laughed.

Because it all made sense; the motive was there at last.

Scandal.

An empire built on chicken soup and fudge recipes

and family cannot endure a scandal. The rest of the world may accept adultery, the jet set and movie stars may be able to screw when and whom they please, but not in the Midwest, not when you're Linda Sue and Ray Springborn, the Kitchen Korner couple.

And who knew how many other Springborn skeletons-in-the-closet Albert would have been able to reveal, *intended* to reveal? Raymond Springborn's mob connections, perhaps? And what else did Linda Sue have to hide from her public? There had to be something. Perhaps any number of somethings. Whatever they were, the scandals would be fueled by their source: the broken-down, pitifully neglected member of the Kitchen Korner clan, Albert Leroy.

"So that's why Albert Leroy had to die," I said.

"He died a long time ago," she said "He was a vegetable."

"Yeah, I know, a potato, you told me before. What did he ask for?"

"He wanted to be vice-president of Springborn-Leroy Enterprises He wanted decision-making power. He wanted a fat salary, like you guessed."

"He wanted too much."

"Yes, he wanted too much! He was a lousy janitor, how could he expect to move into an executive position? He couldn't've handled it, he would have been a public embarrassment to us, if he didn't run us out of business first. He was enough of an embarrassment to us as he was."

"What about that fabled treasure of his?"

"He did have around nine or ten thousand in the bank, left from his inheritance."

"What of that?"

"It's mine now. Or was. I've given you people the equivalent, now that you've been paid twice."

"Shit, that was nice of your brother, wasn't it? Paying you back what it cost to murder him."

"What's the purpose of this? What do you want, Quarry?"

"Nothing. This four thousand will do fine."

"You'll leave, then?"

"I want to know one thing more."

"What?"

"Who is 'Vince'?"

"I have no idea."

"Now don't bullshit me, Linda Sue. Maybe housewives all over middle America would believe you, but this is your brother's killer you're talking to."

"I tell you, I have no idea! I heard Raymond mention the name just now, when you two were talking up in the tower room. I never heard the name mentioned before."

"You realize, don't you, that this 'Vince' is probably the guy who stole the four thousand and killed my partner?"

"What do you care? You have four thousand and you're still alive."

She was right.

"Okay," I said. "I'll be out of Port City before midnight."

"Make it sooner if you can."

"Don't worry. I got no intention of settling down here."

"Quarry…"

"What?"

"Why, uh…why…?"

"Why aren't I twisting your arm for any more than just this four thousand? Because your brother tried the same thing, didn't he? And you murdered him for it. Hell, I'm not even your brother. I'd hate to think what you'd have done to me."

Her eyes and mouth were tight in the plastic surgeon's mask. "You pompous ass…where do you get off with that condescending tone? You keep saying that I murdered my brother. Let me remind you, you smug smart-ass bastard…you murdered Albert Leroy."

"No," I said. "I killed him. You murdered him."

And I left her to think about it. I hoped she'd think about it a long time. But I doubted it.

26

I woke with a start. I looked at my watch. Eight-thirty. I'd slept fifteen minutes. After two hours of staring at the ceiling, thinking more thoughts than is healthy, I'd dropped off to sleep, which wasn't healthy either. When Port City was just another unpleasant memory, then I could sleep. Not now. Not yet.

Peg was beside me, asleep for an hour and a half, an arm draped loose across my midsection, her head snuggled under my shoulder, one breast crushed casually against my side. We'd had supper in the kitchenette and dessert in the bedroom and spent the rest of our time drinking the one-third of a bottle of Scotch which constituted the remainder of her liquor supply and mindlessly chit-chatting, finding out as much about each other as we cared to know.

She gave me an uneasy feeling. All day, being around her had provided a pleasant but nagging sensation, like a dream not quite remembered. It was as though she were a thought in the corner of my mind trying to make itself known, a barely defined reminder of something my mind had long before blocked out. I didn't want to admit what it was, who she indirectly reminded me of. I didn't want those feelings to crawl up out of my subconscious and onto a rock of awareness where they could wriggle and tease and bathe in my understanding of them. I didn't want to face the realization that I hadn't felt like this since I was young, a young man who believed in certain absurd abstract notions, a young man who married before he should have, feeling emotions he defined as profound and should have seen for the animal instincts they were.

But Peg, this sexpot centerfold blonde right out of a wet dream, this gracefully aging beauty who liked one-night stands with greasy-haired potheads ten years her junior, this hard, delicate little broad who screwed me right after she saw me, she was getting dangerously close. She was getting dangerously close to being a person in my life. Women hadn't been persons in my life for a long time. Women were pretty receptacles for pent-up biological and psychological waste material. An extension of self-abuse, nothing more.

But why then was I thinking crazy thoughts about her? Wild thoughts, like thinking of asking her if she could use a business partner, someone who could add a fat bundle of cash to what she'd saved, to aid her in her attempt to either possess or escape from Bunny's. Why was I entertaining the fantasy-insanity of wanting to ask her to go partners with me, to find a bar or club or restaurant or diner or anything somewhere, out west maybe, and run a quiet, legitimate business with days and nights and maybe years of breathing and eating and screwing and doing all those things that make life tolerable, maybe even grow old together, or at least older. Of course I didn't have much saved up, but I did have that plastic bag of white powder that was worth a lot of money, and…

Bullshit.

I was used to being alone. I liked it. People annoyed me. Sometimes companionship got necessary, sure, so you would play some cards with people you could abide, you'd find some good-natured, well-bodied woman and take care of your needs.

But my needs now were shifting. This business of killing, for one thing; this making a life out of death. You can only do that as long as your stomach and head are hard; mine were getting soft in places. I was losing my edge. Otherwise why else would I stick in town after a hit? Detachment, never get personally involved in a job, the fundamental rule, and here I was hip-deep, Boyd's death eating at the back of my head, Albert Leroy less a shadowy target in my mind and more a real person I'd shot in the chest this morning. And the one constant in my life for some years now, the Broker, long-time business associate, had become a person to be distrusted, perhaps feared, at the very least the umbilical cord of our working relationship was soon to be severed, in fact I was…

Goddamnit!

Thinking, I had to stop this goddamn fucking *thinking*!

I slipped out of bed. Peg moaned and reached for me in her sleep but I was too quick for her. I wandered out into the other room, moving through the museum her mother had left behind, went to the window and drew back the curtain. It was raining again.

On the chair by the window was my raincoat and in the raincoat was the nine-millimeter. I'd retrieved the automatic from the trunk of the car since I felt that until I was safely away from Port City it would be best to have gun close at hand. I patted the pocket which held the gun. It was a deep pocket, sewn in special for this purpose. I wished I could put on the coat and go out and find the goddamn man with the goddamn wrench and use the gun on him and leave Port City. There was only one part of this fucking town I'd want to remember, and she was asleep in the other room.

I looked out at the rain. It was coming down damn near straight, coming down heavy, hard, enough so that the gutters of the street were flooding. I looked out at the rain and wondered if I should leave now, while she was still sleeping.

"What are you doing, Quarry?"

I turned and looked at her. She was wearing lacy blue panties and that was all. She was stretching her arms above her head and yawning, her dark nippled breasts flattening as she reached her arms up, blooming full again as she lowered them.

"Nothing," I said.

Outside the thunder rumbled, cracked. She joined me at the window and looked out. The gray streaking rain reflected on her pink flesh, as though someone were projecting a film and using her as a screen. She leaned a knee against the chair and touched the windowsill and said, "I like the rain." She was smiling, but just a little. "I wish I could run out there just like this and jump around in it. Rain like that depresses some people. Not me. It's a release, a gush, like crying, or coming." She leaned over and picked the raincoat up off the chair so she could sit down. The gun fell out of the pocket and dropped to the floor. It was like another crack of thunder. "Christ!" she said, and sat down. She stared at the gun, as though she'd never seen one before and was trying to figure out what it was. Her eyes were very round, very white, like the plates in her mother's china cabinet nearby. Then she looked at me with the blankness that precedes terror, and when her lower lip started to tremble she bit it.

"Easy, Peg," I said. "Now don't get upset."

"Who...who the hell *are* you, Quarry? Who *are* you, for Christ's sake?"

"Now Peg."

"Quarry? Who...what are you doing here?"

"I can explain." I went over and picked the gun up off the floor, shoved it in my belt. "Just take it easy."

I took her by the arm and guided her over to the table in the kitchenette. I held her hand and she said in a soft, frightened but firm little voice, "Just what the hell kind of man are you, anyway?"

I patted her hand and said, conversationally, "What was that man's name? The one in Chicago, the gangster, you called him."

"What...what does that have to do with anything?"

"What was his name?"

"...his name was Frank."

"Frank. Peg, I'm the kind of man your Frank was, I

would guess. You can call it what you want…gangster, mob person, whatever…the label doesn't really matter."

She blinked. Just once. "What are you doing in Port City," she said quickly, almost defiantly. "What are you doing here with me?"

"You really want to know?"

"You tell me, Quarry. You tell me now."

I paused, gathered my thoughts. I said, "I was brought to Port City to carry out a certain task, never mind what. The people I work for have a policy of not telling me why I'm performing a function, or who exactly that function's being performed for. I just do as I'm told, and I'm given money, like any other working stiff. But this time, after the task was carried out, bad things started happening. For openers, almost four thousand dollars that belonged to my partner and me was stolen, and that was the nicest thing that happened to us. Then somebody murdered my partner and hung around and tried to murder me. You've noticed the bruised area on my chest and shoulder?"

She didn't answer right away. Her face had turned bloodless white when I mentioned murder, but after a moment she managed to nod her head yes.

"That was from where somebody tried to do me in with a wrench. Damn near succeeded, too. So I been nosing around, asking questions, looking under beds. I'm at a dead end right now. I wanted to find the guy who worked the wrench on my partner, and then on me, but I'm at a dead end. So now I'm going to throw in my cards, cash in my chips and look for another game."

"Does this have anything to do with the Springborns?"

"I'd rather not say. The less you know about the specifics, the safer you are. All I can tell you is I was looking to find the man responsible for killing my partner and stealing my money."

"And if you would have found the...man responsible?"

"Let's just say he would've paid what he owes me. You wouldn't want to know the details."

She shuddered slightly. "No. I wouldn't." She paused for a moment, pulled her hand out from under mine. "What about us. Quarry? What about you and me?"

"I won't pretend our meeting was accidental. You knew about some people I wanted to get at. I managed to find out in an underhanded way some of the things I needed to know."

The color came back to her cheeks. "And getting into my pants was sort of a bonus for you, then, wasn't it?"

"Peg."

"I'm a tour guide providing sex on the side, right? That's what I am to you, that's all I am to you."

I said, "It could've been that way. Things worked out different."

"Did they?" Her face was emotionless—motionless—but I thought I could see something starting to melt in her eyes.

"Peg," I said, "remember what you said this morning? Remember what you said about being able to tell somebody in twenty years all about what we did together, making love together? Well so could I. Twenty years from now I'll remember every detail of being with you. You just look me up in twenty years and try me."

She gave me a tentative smile. She said, "Will you, Quarry?"

"Yes I will," I said.

She was quiet for a moment; she was thinking. Then she made her decision. She said, "Okay. So you're a bastard. You're a son of a bitch and a bastard but I can live with it." She grinned. "Who knows? Maybe I just got a thing for men with guns."

"Maybe so."

"Quarry?"

"Yes, Peg?"

"Have you given up on finding the man responsible?"

"Pretty much."

"You don't want to give up, though, do you?"

"No. I'm close to him. I'm very close."

"Can I help you?"

"I don't want to involve you any deeper in this."

"Aren't there any questions you could ask me? That isn't involvement, not really. There's no risk in me answering a few questions."

"Well…"

"Please."

I stopped. Then I said, "Do you know anybody named Vince?"

She gave me an odd look, cocking her head to one side.

"Vince," I repeated. "A guy named Vince."

"He wouldn't be a cab driver, would he?"

I thought for a moment. What was it Springborn had said? Something about Vince driving a hack and making a lot of money? "He might be," I said.

"That'd be Carol's brother, then."

Carol's brother? Carol? That was the other name Springborn had mentioned! And was that the name Boyd had used, the name of the woman he was "subletting" the apartment from?

"Who is Carol?" I said. Knowing the answer.

"The girl I told you about this morning. My friend. The one Ray Springborn was shacking up with, then all of a sudden sent packing to Florida."

It was making sense. It was starting to make a lot of sense. I said, "Tell me about Vince."

She shrugged. "He's a deadbeat, and that's the whole story. He drives a cab, thanks to Ray. Carol asked Ray to fix him up with a good job and Ray agreed. Besides, it keeps Vince's mouth shut about Ray and Carol. Matter of fact, I think Vince might've been putting the squeeze on Ray just lately, maybe that's why Ray sent Carol down to Florida for a while." She shook her head. "Why Carol cares about that brother of hers is a mystery to me, but I suppose it's because he's all the family she's got around here. You see, their parents are split up, divorced, and moved away long ago. That Vince is a real shit, Quarry. He's queer as hell, too."

"What?"

"He's queer. They even had him in jail for it."

I remembered what Springborn had said, the implication in his words...*hasn't he tried anything?* Springborn had said. *You don't go for that stuff, do you?*

"Actually," Peg was saying, "I guess he wasn't jailed for being a queer exactly, it was something worse than that. Much worse, because Christ knows as far as I'm concerned a person's sex life is his own business, but this Vince...he's a pervert in the true sense of the word. You know why he got thrown in jail? He was propositioning other homosexuals, especially guys passing through town, you know? He'd take them out in the country in his cab and roll them. Take every cent they had, even their clothes sometimes, and beat the crap out of them for the sheer pleasure of it."

I understood.

I understood it all.

Boyd, I said silently, *Boyd wherever you are, you son of a lesbian bitch, wherever you are, you're an asshole. A dead one, but an asshole.* Why hadn't it occurred to me? The obvious! The dead obvious fact that Boyd had been slipping lately, that Boyd was getting sloppy in his work, so sloppy bad I was thinking serious of quitting him. But he had been even more stupid than I'd given him credit for. He'd been stupid enough, asshole-dumb enough, out-of-his-fucking-mind crazy enough to get involved in one of his gay flings *while on a job!*

That broken heart he'd been nursing, that busted heart he'd been carrying around with him as a souvenir of his disintegrating personal life, that torn valentine he wore in his chest he'd tried to paste back together with a new love, a love he found for himself right here in Port City.

And Boyd had picked himself a dandy lover. I could picture the first meeting in my mind. Because I knew what Vince looked like, I was sure of it. I was sure he was that clown in the taxi stand this morning, the guy who'd sidled up to me in the Port City Taxi Service this very damn morning! I could see him in my mind, a skinny guy in a white T-shirt (though in the apartment it had been a black one, hadn't it?) dark complexioned, his hair oily and curly and black, his smile leering with the tooth in front chipped, his voice tough one second, effeminate the next. I could see him talking to Boyd, while Boyd thumbed through *Twilight Love* at the paperback rack.

I'd been right about one thing: it *was* an inside job. Vince was the brother of Carol, the girl who'd been staying in the apartment where Boyd was doing lookout, meaning Vince knew enough about the situation to know that Boyd and I had been brought to town to do some kind of Springborn dirty work; it was unlikely he'd have it figured right down to the murder of Albert Leroy, but he knew that Boyd and I were in town to do something under-the-table for one of the Springborns, though he no doubt assumed Raymond, but never mind that. Vince had probably been able to gather from Boyd that a large amount of money was involved, and Boyd had probably promised Vince some of that money. Might even have indicated when the money would become available. Might even have arranged one last rendezvous with the chipped-tooth charmer before leaving town.

I had the sudden urge to go back to that alley where I'd left Boyd behind a wall of garbage cans and see if the body was still there. If it was, I'd kick it in the ass.

Peg was staring at me, watching my eyes move with thought. When I came out of my near-trance, she said, "Is Vince the man...responsible?"

The man responsible? The man with the wrench? The man who killed Boyd? Who took my money? Who tried to murder me? Yes. Yes he was.

"Never mind," I said.

"Do you want to know where he lives?" she said.

I nodded.

"Above the cab stand," she said "There's a wooden stairway in back. It's the only apartment up there. He's got the whole floor to himself. He makes good money driving a cab. Thanks to Ray."

"Thank you, Peg."

"It's okay."

"Now forget all about it."

"I already have."

"Good."

"Quarry?"

"Yes?"

"Are you going now?"

"I better."

"Are you leaving Port City?"

"Yes."

"Right now?"

"Soon."

"Will I see you again?"

"Not tonight."

"When?"

"Not tonight."

"I'll…hear from you, then?"

"You'll hear from me."

"Quarry."

"Yes, Peg."

"Come with me for a minute."

"Yes, Peg."

27

The same woman was sitting behind the glass counter, but she was wearing a different dress; she had traded in the red-and-white check for a blue-and-white, which was draped over her heavyset frame like a pup tent without poles. Her hair didn't look quite so frowzy this time, which probably meant she'd just come on during the past hour or so, whereas on my last visit to the Port City Taxi Service I must've caught her at the tail end of her tour of duty.

"How's she goin', mister?" she said, her smile a fold in the layered flesh of her face. She puffed at the last inch of a cigarette and flashed a brown grin and said, "What can I do you for?"

"Hi," I said. "Hell of a night."

"Hell of a night is right. Miserable as hell."

"Yeah, all that damn rain. Listen, is Vince working tonight?"

"Vince? Sure, he went on an hour ago. You want me to get him on the squawker for you?"

"No, don't bother. Just wondered what shift he was working."

"He don't get done till early this mornin' after dawn."

"He very busy tonight?"

"She comes in spurts. Right now he is. He's backed up four or five calls. But if you want to see him, just take a load off and wait. He stops in for coffee every hour or so, when he gets a slow spell. He'll be along as soon as these calls is done, give him a half hour, forty-five minutes."

"Well, I'll come back in a little while."

"Suit yourself."

I bought a package of gum from her and swapped her smiles and went out the door and stood in the soaking rain. The night was particularly dark, the street lamps like flashlights in a huge dark warehouse. The street was full of rain and empty of cars. Only in the taverns a block down (Albert Leroy's block) were there signs of life, but even the drinking crowd seemed intimidated by the dreary weather, the noise and jukebox music of the bars seeming muted, half-hearted. Up here, by the taxi stand, all was quiet, deserted.

I walked around to the back, passing Boyd's green Mustang, and put on my gloves and got the nine-millimeter automatic firmly in hand. I climbed the open wooden stairway up to where Vince kept his apartment and got to work on his door. It had a new-style lock that might have been designed by a moonlighting burglar, the type of lock you can use a credit card to open. Once inside I pulled the shades in the kitchen and switched on the light and for a moment I was startled. For that moment I thought I was back where Boyd had stayed, back in that apartment I'd since found out belonged to somebody named Carol —the same pink stucco walls, the same new but cheap

furniture like something you'd see in a middle-grade
mobile home; the wall-to-wall carpeting was even the
same color, a murky green. The layout of the apartment
was identical to the other one and it was obvious the ren-
ovations of both had been handled by the same contractor. Which wasn't surprising considering Vince and
his sister Carol shared the same landlord in Raymond
Springborn.

Vince was not a neat housekeeper. Any fears I might
have had about coming in from the rain and leaving a
tell-tale mess behind were quickly dispelled. The kitchen
table was a sea of empty beer bottles and cans (mostly
Budweiser) with more of the same littered around the
edges of the room; the sink was full of several days' dishes
and the smell of garbage was so strong I wanted to wrap
the whole room in brown paper and put it out for the
trash. The bedroom's focal point was its unmade bed, its
sheets soiled and smelly and sticky-damp. Underwear
and dirty socks and colored T-shirts and jeans were wadded
and tossed here and there, as though Vince took off his
clothes like a greedy kid unwrapping a Christmas present. On the bedroom walls were stuck various clipped-
out pictures from porno mags, though nothing outright
obscene: muscle men parading around in jocks, and lots
of women showing lots, but nothing frontal below the
waist. Vince's taste did seem evenly divided between men
and women, so the boy wasn't strictly gay, and he wasn't
particularly kinky either, from the look of the pics on the
wall; no whips or chains or that. Vince seemed to like his

perversion kept within certain limits of good taste, and there was no real indication of a penchant for violence, though I later found some karate books in his closet, mixed in with automotive magazines, books and magazines on body-building and some "swinging singles" publications. The living room was better ordered than the rest of the place, probably because the only furniture was a sofa and a color television, the rest of the room being as empty as I imagined Vince's mind and personality to be. Oh there were a few, just a few, scattered beer cans and bottles, and a half-eaten sack of corn curls and mostly eaten cup of clam dip on the floor by the sofa. A very mild, unimpressive mess after the kitchen and bedroom, which were the work of a virtuoso slob. The only other room in the apartment was the bathroom, which I'd rather not go into.

In the bedroom, in the closet behind the double sliding doors, under the stack of books and magazines, I found a spot in the corner where the carpeting could be pulled back and two loose boards easily lifted up and out and a cubbyhole revealed, and down in the cubbyhole, wrapped in a black T-shirt, was the money and the wrench.

I counted the money and it was all there. I examined the wrench. He'd scrubbed it down clean, but had kept it, and kept it hidden, like the moronic amateur he was. I looked at the T-shirt. I set the nine-millimeter on the floor so I could take the shirt in my hands and rip it in half. After that I felt better.

And then I put the money down into the deep raincoat

pocket. The wrench I stuck in my belt and I put the torn T-shirt back down in the cubbyhole, replaced the boards, patted the carpet back in place, restacked the books and magazines, picked up the automatic and left the apartment.

Out on the landing I took off my gloves, found room in the deep pocket for both money and automatic, and walked down the wooden steps and into the taxi stand parking lot, where I transferred the money and wrench to the trunk of Boyd's car. Then I went back into the taxi stand to wait for Vince.

Fifteen minutes later he came in. Strutted in. He liked himself. A lot. His jeans were tight and worn down around the hips, his skinny arms tattooed and wiry-muscled, hanging from his short-sleeve red T-shirt like plastic tubing, his hair was greased back like he just heard of James Dean and if I'd had a motorcycle I could have sold it to him. He said, "Shitty night," to the woman behind the counter.

"Shitty weather, you mean?" she asked him, working on another stub of a cigarette. "Or shitty fares?"

"Shitty everything," he said.

"Guy at the back table wants to see you. Been waiting, acts like he knows you."

"Yeah?" He leaned over to whisper, though he knew I could still hear him. "Who the hell is the bastard?"

"Oh, he's been around here before. Just this mornin' he rented some parking space from me."

Vince shrugged and strolled over and got himself a

cup of coffee and leaned against the counter and watched me. When he'd finished his coffee, he rooster-walked up to where I was sitting and sat next to me, close, and gave me his best chipped-tooth smile. He said, "Do I know you, Jack?"

My guess was he didn't. We'd met twice before: once in that apartment, when he introduced me to his wrench; and again early this morning, when he approached me in his girlie voice. When he'd gone into that swish number this morning, I hadn't recognized him; I didn't figure he'd recognized me, either. It had been dark scuffling in that apartment, very dark, and my guess was he hadn't seen me any better than I'd seen him.

"I was in here this morning," I said, "remember? You were acting kind of cute." I kept a hard edge in my voice to let him know I wasn't back to see him because I found his body attractive.

He remembered. He got suddenly nervous, squirming in his seat, and he laughed, a coughing sort of laugh, and scratched his head. Waving his hands, avoiding direct eye contact with me, he said, "I was just putting you on, Jack. Do I look like some kind of goddamn fag?"

"No," I said. "No you don't."

"So what do you want, anyhow?"

"I want to know if you're interested in making some money."

His smart-ass grin crawled over onto the left side of his face. He said, "I dunno, I dunno, Jack. I had me a… better than average couple days, you might say."

"Piss." I shook my head. "How much can you make driving a cab?"

He kept grinning, eyes twinkling with all sorts of private knowledge. "Just so happens you caught me when I'm not that bad off, Jack. So whatever your hustle is I ain't interested."

"You should be."

"Oh should I be? I see. Suppose you tell me why *you* should be interested in *me*? I ain't in the blowjob business, if that's what you're here for."

I put on an indignant look and said, tightly, "Maybe I'm talking to the wrong guy. The guy I wanted was supposed to be a real hardass. I asked around to find just the right kind of guy, and they tell me, see Vince, this guy at the cab station, and I say, shit, I ran into that guy already, he's a fucking queer, and they say, don't let him fool you, that's how he makes side money, rolling queers and generally hardassing it around. And they say this Vince isn't afraid of doing anything, anything that's got good money tied up to it somehow."

He rubbed his chin. He wasn't nervous anymore. He studied me for a moment, then said, "Maybe you got sent to the wrong place."

"Yeah?"

And then the cocky little bastard wagged his head side to side and grinned wide and said, "Yeah, and maybe you got sent to the right place, only it just ain't open for business at the time being, so forget it." He stood up.

"I pay big and ask little."

"Forget it, Jack."

"One hour of your time."

"Just forget it."

"One thousand bucks."

That caught him on one foot. He swallowed. His expression settled into a blank stare, which I took to be concentration. He sat back down. Then he started to nod. He was nodding more emphatically by the time he said, "Let's go outside and talk. We can sit in my cab."

I said, "Fine," and followed him outside. The rain was easing up, but it was still insistent. We both were wet by the time we were sitting in the front seat of his cab. He was excited, his breath fogging up the windows right off.

"One thousand fucking bucks, Jack?"

"That's right."

"Times is good for me now, but even in good times I can use that kind of bread."

"Who can't?"

"But money that big, whew! Hell, Jack, that's got to mean trouble, and I don't know you from Adam, I don't know you from shit, I don't know period."

"The less you know the better."

"Fuck that shit, Jack! You can tell me what the hell's going on or you can stuff the thousand. You haven't even told me what the hell it is you want me to do."

"All I want from you is one thing. One simple thing. I want you to drive a car for me. I want you to deliver a car."

"A thousand bucks to deliver a car?"

"This car is special…what it's carrying is special. The

people you deliver it to will take the car to a garage and strip it down immediately and get the stuff they're after."

He smiled, tense, not showing his chipped tooth. He knew what I was talking about. He all but said, "Narcotics." He wanted to say it. But he restrained himself. Finally he said, "Okay, Jack, but why me? You got a load of…Jesus, a load like that, and you ask a stranger's help? You must be fucking desperate."

"I am. I'm desperate."

"What the hell's the situation, anyway?"

"Well…" I made a show of weighing the consequences of telling him "the truth." With mock reluctance I said, "My partner and I were making this run, and last night he took sick. Terrible sick. This was an overnight stop for us, so I figured by morning he'd be okay. But he got worse, much worse."

"What was wrong with him?"

"I don't know, food poisoning maybe, or some weird-ass virus. All I know is he's practically dying. This infection or something hit him all at once, hit him out of nowhere, and now I need a driver. To complete the run. What do you say?"

"He's too sick to drive?"

"I'm asking you, aren't I?"

"That's just it, it's so crazy, you asking me."

"Who the hell else can I ask in this damn hick town? You got to bail me out, Vince. The money's good. Do it."

"When is it, this delivery?"

"Midnight."

"Shit, it's after eleven now. Where we got to be?"

"The quarry on the river road, just outside Davenport."

He was nodding his head, starting to buy it. He said, "We could make that, easy."

"Good. You take the lead and I'll follow you. After you deliver the car, I'll drive you back to Port City." I got a roll of bills out from my pocket, part of the money Mrs. Springborn had given me. I peeled off five bills, all of them hundreds, and tossed them in his blue-jeaned lap. He stared down at them. "Five more like that," I told him, "when the job's over."

He thought about it. He scratched his oily head and said, to himself, "This has been a day," then to me, "Let's get going, Jack."

"Right," I said.

We shook hands.

28

The river road followed the Mississippi's edge faithfully, and no doubt provided much visual pleasure for folks out on sunny afternoon outings. On the one side of the road, cottages dotted the river shore; on the other side, a high green bluff was strung with all sorts of houses, from modest to lavish, mutually enjoying the scenic view. After ten miles or so the bluff dwindled and the ground became flat and fenced off, the rich farmland Iowa is known for; on the other side of the road the cottages had given way to thick forest-like clumps of trees. At times the road rolled up hills, one of them peaking and leveling out to provide an overview of the river from a breathtaking highpoint, while on the road's left was a sheer cliff-like wall of rock, like something out of Colorado or Wyoming. Other times the road swung down through valley-nestled villages, quiet, sheltered little worlds removed from this era. The river road was a Sunday driver's paradise, the scenery varied and having more slices of America along it than any single stretch of twenty-five-mile road you can think of. At midnight, in the rain, it was a fucking nightmare.

I was staying a quarter mile behind Vince because I didn't want him to get a good look at the car I was driving. I'd hustled him into my rental Ford and after he'd taken off I had followed in Boyd's green Mustang. I figured there was some chance Vince would recognize the Mustang as Boyd's and I didn't want him tipping to who I was or what I was doing. On the other hand, I didn't want to let him get out of my sight. Out of my reach. So I had to stay right with him, without tailgating him.

He'd questioned me about why I was trusting him with the delivery of the cargo-laden car, and I had to explain it six ways to get him to accept it. I kept inventing reasons and he kept shuffling and saying, "I dunno, Jack," and then finally he said he guessed it made sense to him that I'd want him in front of me where I could see him, rather than in back where he could quietly disappear with my five hundred bucks and a car provided by me. Such a contingency he could comprehend, because it and every other crooked-ass possibility had occurred to him: Vince wasn't smart, but he had a mind that twisted in those kind of patterns.

So everything was fine until he suggested he'd run up to his apartment and stash the five hundred and grab his windbreaker since he might have to stand out in the rain a while. Before that could develop into a problem, I threw my raincoat around his shoulders (pockets empty of course, the nine-millimeter in the front seat of the Mustang, under a newspaper) and pushed him into the rental Ford and bid him bon voyage.

The Mustang took the choppy old road badly, its suspension system outclassed by this patchwork quilt of concrete chunks. When things would get less bumpy, when a smooth stretch would show out of nowhere, the wetness of the pavement made driving all the more treacherous.

Up ahead Vince fishtailed the Ford a couple times hitting slick spots like that, and he wasn't doing over fifty-five. I felt myself start to slide once or twice. Just when the road would seem to be evening out for good, up would come a water-filled pothole big enough to do the backstroke in.

I glanced down and saw the odometer had clocked twenty-one miles since leaving Port City. The quarry would be coming round soon. I crouched over the steering wheel and peered out through the windshield as the wipers swished back and forth.

The half-dozen buildings were huddled together like conspirators. Three of the buildings were cylindrical, resembling silos, and made of cement; the rest were gray ribbed-steel obelisks with smokestacks pouring out pure white smoke, puffy clouds as white as innocence, dissipating as the rain got to them. A black shaft slanted across the highway from one of the obelisks to a Quonset hut, the shaft housing the conveyer that brought the limestone from the quarry to the cement processing plant.

The quarry itself was immense. Even in the darkness of the rainy night, partially lit as I passed through the compound of buildings, I could see across to the other side and the damn thing looked like the Grand Canyon, only older, its limestone ledges having a barren, dead beauty. The depth of it varied from probably fifty feet in places to one-hundred and fifty. It covered acres, hundreds of acres, and it was long, extending a mile past the smoke-exuding plant, where a skeleton crew was continuing through the night, transforming the cold, brittle rock into sacks of cement.

Broker had said two cars would be waiting for me, one of them to take me back to Port City. There was only one car, a dark blue Dodge Charger, its motor running. That was no surprise, but it was a solid confirmation: any slight doubt of Broker's intentions dissolved like the smoke rising into the rain. I watched Vince pull the Ford over and, after hanging back for a minute, I drove on past both cars, like somebody who was just happening along. Half a mile later I cut my lights and U-turned and came back slow. When I got within an eighth of a mile I let the car crawl quietly off to the side of the road and got out. There were some bushes lining the fence that edged the quarry, and they hid me as I moved quickly along, careful not to brush against them.

I had told Vince to sit in the car and wait for three minutes, to give me a chance to do what I had just done. The nine-millimeter was tight in my gloved hand and I was close by when Vince got out of the Ford and began to approach the dark blue Charger.

Visibility was very low, but I saw what happened clearly, as I was only a few feet away.

The two cars were parked parallel to each other, forming right angles with the road, but there was half a block distance between the two cars and Vince walked so slowly it seemed it would take him forever to near the Charger. Hands deep in the pockets of my raincoat, Vince baby-stepped toward the car and had cut the distance in half when the window on the driver's side of the Charger rolled down. An arm extended from the open window. Vince stopped. He saw the gun pointed directly at him and he turned to move and the thud of a silenced automatic made a barely perceptible addition to the sounds of the wet night. Vince clutched his side. He fell to his knees. I couldn't tell how bad the wound was, but my guess was it wasn't fatal; he was moving too good, very good for a man crawling on his knees.

The door flew open on the Charger. A slender figure in a dark coat jumped from the car, limped frantically toward Vince, who was clawing through the mud and gravel toward the Ford. The slender man caught up with Vince without much trouble. He bent over, saying, "All right, Quarry, you bastard, this is going to be a goddamn pleasure," and he turned Vince over and lifted him up by the raincoat lapels and realized it wasn't me.

He dropped Vince back to the muddy wet ground. "Christ!" Carl said, and I hit him behind the left ear with the barrel of the nine-millimeter.

Carl went down face first, splashing into a puddle. He landed just to Vince's left.

I took the silenced automatic from Carl's limp finger-tips and stuck the gun in my belt. Vince sat there and watched me with his mouth open, his face a mixture of pain and incredulity and stupidity, the rain running down his forehead and over his face like a combination of tears and slobber. He looked at me hard, squinching his eyes, and then he got mad. But before he said anything, he scooched back on his ass toward the Ford, till he was leaning safely against the fender of the car, which gave him a little, not much, but a little breathing room from the unconscious Carl.

Vince sputtered, his mouth full of rain, and perhaps blood. He said, "You, you fucking son of a bitch, you, you goddamn son of a fucking bitch…I'm shot, Jesus I'm shot, that shit shot me…no trouble, you said, easiest money I ever made you said…"

"Shut up," I said.

The narrowed eyes went suddenly wide, and wild, and he said, "What are you gonna do, what are you gonna do for me? You gotta do something for me…you're not going to leave me bleed? Huh? Huh? I'm hurt, Christ Jesus I'm hurt, but I know I can make it if you just help me—you're gonna help me aren't you?"

"You be quiet. You be quiet and maybe I'll help you."

"But…"

"Sit there and relax. Don't panic or shock'll set in. Don't waste your energy or you'll go unconscious. Just sit there and stay cool."

"But…"

I raised the automatic and he shut up. Or almost shut up. He was whimpering, but not loud enough to be annoying.

Carl was starting to rouse. I helped him. I poked his ribs with my foot.

"Up," I said.

Carl groaned. He rolled around in the puddle and got his nose deep down in the water and he started choking and coughing and flapping his arms. He pushed up on his hands and made wedges in the soft ground and hobbled onto his feet. Or foot. There was mud hanging on his face like melting gelatin.

"How's it going, Carl?"

Carl swallowed and it didn't taste good. He said, "You double-crossing son of a bitch!" His voice was strained, and almost shrill.

"I'd laugh at that," I said, "if I thought we had time to be funny."

"You're dead, Quarry. You're a dead man."

"No. Not the case. Had Broker sent somebody competent out here to kill me, somebody with two legs and a brain, I might be dead. But I'm not."

"The Broker..."

"The Broker is home cozy and warm in his bed. He wouldn't bother coming out here. He doesn't dirty himself with this sort of thing."

Carl wiped off his face and stood very still. Like he was at attention, or facing a firing squad or something. He said, "Go ahead, Quarry. Get it over with."

"Get what over with? You think I'm going to kill you? You aren't worth killing, you gimpy asshole."

"What...what are you going to do?"

"I'm going to send you home to Broker. I'm going to let you limp back over to your shiny new Dodge Charger and roar into the sunset."

He was frozen with disbelief.

I said, "Go back to Broker. Shoo."

"What's this...what's this all about?"

"Go back to Broker, Carl. But one thing...bring him back here."

"What? You're crazy."

"Get him up and bring him out here and let him get his ass wet like the rest of us."

"You're out of your mind."

"You got forty minutes. Broker doesn't live all that far from here. I'll wait forty minutes. Now go."

"Go?"

"Go."

"Sure," Carl said, humoring me, "fine. I'll bring him back in forty minutes."

"I know you will. Just tell him one thing for me. You tell him I only gave him half that load of heroin from the airport job. You tell him I kept back a bag. Tell him I got it hid safely away, and if he wants the key to where I hid it, he should come back here within forty minutes and bring twenty thousand in hundreds with him."

Carl didn't argue with me. He didn't try to tell me Broker wouldn't be able to raise the money or other similar lies. Twenty thousand was a low figure for the stuff, very low, and I only picked that figure because I knew Broker would have that much on hand at home.

Carl said, "I'll be back in forty minutes with the Broker." Carl knew the Broker would come; for the heroin, Broker would come.

"Go, Carl."

Carl nodded. Very carefully, very slowly, he sloshed back to the Charger, its motor still running. He waited at the door for any last instructions I might have I said, "You come back with him, Carl. Don't bring anyone else. Come unarmed."

Carl nodded again, got in the car and pulled out. I watched the Charger disappear into the rain and seconds later the road was deserted again.

Behind me, Vince said, weakly, "What…what's this about? Who…who the hell are you?"

I turned and looked at him. He looked pitiful. A skinny shot-up kid in my raincoat, leaning against the Ford and clutching his side. His long hair was hanging in thick wet streaks across his forehead, making a stark contrast with his pale white face. His mouth was slack open, the chipped tooth giving him a look of naive idiocy.

I said, "You don't know, do you?"

Vince said nothing.

I said nothing.

We waited.

Vince said, "In Christ's name, do something…help me…I'll fucking bleed to death if you don't do something…"

I just looked at him.

He said, "You got to, got to…please…oh, please, please, do something…"

He was right. It was time to do something.

I said, "All right. I got a first-aid kit in the trunk of my car. I'll go get it."

He made a strange sound, a cross between a whimper and a sigh. He whispered, "Thanks…thanks, Jack."

I walked the eighth of a mile back to the Mustang and opened the trunk.

I got out the wrench.

29

"Shit," Carl said. He paced awkwardly back and forth, like he was trying to make fun of himself. He'd been fifty minutes bringing Broker out here and I'd told him forty. He'd come back and found the area deserted and for a full minute now he'd been pacing and saying shit. He didn't know I'd moved the two cars to where they couldn't be seen. The rental Ford was at the mouth of the gravel access road to the quarry, the car just barely out of view, where I could get to it quick if I had to. Boyd's Mustang was down in the quarry itself, not far from what was left of Vince.

Carl looked at Broker, whose face was visible in the back side window of the car. Carl held out the palms of his hands as if to say, "What can I do?" Broker pursed his lips and shrugged with his eyebrows. Carl shook his head as if to say, "I'm sorry." Broker eased the irritation from his face and nodded forgiveness.

Just the same, Carl went back to his pacing alongside the car, which this trip was not the shiny dark blue Charger, but a big brown Buick with a vinyl top. Broker's car, obviously. An executive's car.

"Shit," Carl said again, "shit, shit, shit."

"Oh stop crying," I said. I stepped out from the bushes

and let Carl see I was still keeping company with the nine-millimeter.

Relief flooded Carl's face, and then anger. Carl spoke and his voice dripped venom, but his words were contrite: "I'm…I'm sorry I was late."

"It's okay," I said. "Open your coat."

He unbuttoned the black raincoat and held it open. I walked over to him and gave him a quick, one-handed frisk. He was unarmed. "Good boy," I said. "That fake leg of yours isn't hollowed out and full of firecrackers, now is it?"

Carl pouted. His eyes told me to go to hell. But he said nothing.

"You can close your coat now," I said.

"Where's your friend," Carl asked.

He meant Vince.

At the bottom of this limestone pit, Carl, where he landed when I shoved his remains over the edge.

"I patched him up," I said, "and he's doing fine. Walking up and down the road here, keeping his eyes open. Making sure you and Broker didn't bring any of your friends along."

Carl said, "Broker wants you to get in the car and talk with him in there."

I waved the gun toward Broker, whose face in the window of the Buick was bland and emotionless and practically bored. "Broker," I said, loud, "get your ass out here!"

The back door opened. Broker didn't come out, but his voice did. He said, "Climb in here with me, Quarry. No need to stand out in the rain and catch pneumonia."

"Why don't you come out here and join me, Broker. I been in the rain so long it's gotten to be my natural state."

"Please," the Broker said. With solemn patience.

"Why not," I said. I looked at Carl and said, "You get in the front. Sit on the rider's side and don't cause any trouble."

Carl did as he was told.

Broker was wearing a charcoal double-knit suit and a dark blue shirt and a wide tie colored robin's egg blue. He moved over to make room for me, which put him directly behind Carl. There was plenty of room in the Buick's backseat—headroom, legroom, everything. I laid the nine-millimeter on my lap and folded my gloved hands. It was cold in the car. The damn air conditioner was on, which was stupid on a rainy and not particularly warm night like this one, and between its coldness and size, that Buick could've been used as a meat locker.

"Excuse the delay," Broker said. "My wife and I were entertaining a houseful of guests, and it was most difficult getting away."

"Having a party, huh, Broker? Well that's one way to establish an alibi."

"Please, Quarry." His mustache quivered.

"You and your pretty wife are eating caviar and sipping cocktails and I'm out here in the rain getting my nuts shot off by a cripple."

I could see Carl in the rearview mirror. I could see his face get tense. But he didn't say anything.

I said, "You might be interested to know that my business in Port City has been settled, and without rousing the police or causing J. Edgar Hoover to rise from the dead."

Broker's expression turned grim. He nodded slowly and said, "I received a call from the party who contracted your services…"

"Mrs. Springborn, you mean."

Broker couldn't keep back the sharp look this time. But it passed quickly. He said, "The party informed me of your visit, and that you had promised to leave Port City."

"That's right."

"And that you demanded and were paid an additional four thousand dollars. How do you think that makes me look? I'm not a blackmailer, Quarry, I won't condone extortion."

I didn't know whether to laugh at the bastard or strangle him. I told him so.

"Quarry, please!" The Broker patted his hands at the air. "Please. I shouldn't have brought up the subject." He cleared his throat. "My friend, we could drag this out forever, shouting at each other, accusing each other of all sorts of things. You could tell me again of your distaste for that job at the airport, and reexpress your general displeasure with my management of your affairs these past several months. And I could remind you again of your unpardonable behavior in Port City, and, successful or not, could you really refute the insanity of staying on the scene after a job and, in the name of God, investigating? I think not. This is unfortunate, this is all most unfortunate, and rehashing all of our grievances will get us nowhere. I'm sorry our mutually beneficial working arrangement must be dissolved in so disagreeable a way, after so long a period of time. It's obvious reconciliation is impossible. I'm fond of you, I really am, and you've done good work for me. But in recent days we've treated each other badly and have left our relationship in a state of damage beyond repair. Tonight, and I admit my judgment was faulty, tonight I tried to have you killed. Just as you, while working for me, betrayed our trust and kept for yourself valuable property belonging to me. Well, one hand washes the other, as they say, and I say let us dispense with past differences and get on with the business at hand."

If he'd been running for something, I would've voted for him. The rain beat on the roof of the car like applause.

"Well, Quarry?"

"Okay," I said.

The Broker nodded gravely and withdrew from his inside suitcoat pocket a thick, sealed envelope. He ripped the envelope open with a great sense of the dramatic, and displayed the thickness of green bills.

I dug into my pants pocket for the key. I handed it to him.

He said, "The airport? A locker at the airport?"

I nodded.

"Reckless," the Broker said, softly, "most reckless."

He handed me the envelope, without ceremony this time. I spread it open, ran my thumb across the edges of the bills. The bills were new and crisp; they even smelled new. I started to count the money, and from the corner of my eye I saw the Broker make a movement of his head and in the rearview mirror I saw Carl nod back.

And I saw that the glove compartment was open.

Sometime during Broker's pompous speech, Carl had quietly opened the glove compartment.

Carl was watching me in the mirror to make sure I wasn't watching him. I waited until his hand was inside the glove compartment and on the revolver and then I grabbed Broker by the arm and yanked him over hard and plastered myself against the door and Carl fired.

Carl fired and his bullet caught Broker in the right eye and the back of Broker's head flew off and sprayed-splattered a surrealistic, mostly scarlet design across the back window.

There was a moment when it could have been over for me. Broker had fallen on me, a thousand pounds of dead Broker had fallen on my lap and I couldn't get to the automatic, but somehow I shoved Broker over toward the other door and got my hands on the gun and brought it up to return fire.

I should have been dead by that time, but Carl had hesitated; he had hesitated and let his mind get in front of his reflexes. He had hesitated and had had time to realize what happened, to see through the smoke and red mist, to see Broker's ghastly mutilated face, and Carl knew what he had done, and the look of horror on his face lasted only a fraction of an instant, because that was when the nine-millimeter came mercifully up and rested against his cheek and kissed his face into nothing at all.

Fingers fumbling, I unlocked the door, jerked the latch, rolled out of the car, gratefully crawled into the muddy gravel, choking on the smell of cordite, ears ringing from the explosion of Carl's unsilenced revolver going off in the confines of the car.

My instinct was to leave immediately, just get the hell out. I got to the Ford and inside and drove up out of the quarry access road and by the time I was back onto the open area where the Buick was parked, the engine still purring, I had decided on a course of action. I guess it had been in my mind all along. If I'd been honest with myself, I would have admitted that my relationship with the Broker couldn't have ended any other way. But I hadn't faced the truth. I'd waited for the inevitable situation to come around, and had met it as though it were a surprise.

I placed my nine-millimeter automatic in Broker's limp hand. I put Vince's wrench under the front seat of the Buick. The investigating team would have a merry time sorting it all out. They'd get as far as a crossfire between Broker and Carl and then would face a maze leading at one turn to a locker in the Quad City Airport, a locker with a little plastic bag full of heroin in it, leading into an even vaster labyrinth of mob activity. Another turn of the maze would lead back to Port City and Boyd's corpse and Albert Leroy and maybe even the Springborns. But not me. I'd be gone. Like I'd never been there.

I didn't like leaving the nine-millimeter behind like that. The gun had been with me for a long time. But then so had Broker, and I was leaving a lot of things behind at the stone quarry on the river road.

30

A pretty girl in a yellow bikini was running and I didn't see her. She bumped into me as I was getting out of my Opel GT and knocked me down. Her hair was long and just a shade lighter yellow than the bikini. She helped me up and smiled, her white teeth accented by the darkness of her tan, and excused herself. I told her not to worry about it and she smiled again and said that's a nice car you have. I returned her smile and watched her bounce off, going on ahead to meet her boyfriend, who was waiting up by the penny arcade for her. They joined hands and, in step with each other, crossed the street and disappeared into the swarm of flesh on the beach.

Late August is a frantic time around Twin Lakes. The high school and college kids seem desperate to get every last drop of sun-and-fun squeezed out of the dying summer. I wasn't moving near so fast, but then I didn't have to start back to school after the weekend.

I'd come to the arcade hoping to play some pool, but the place was all but empty. It was too clear and hot a day to waste in here, for the kids anyway; the front end of the arcade was open to the street, with the beach just across the way, and a breeze blowing in from the lake was enough to keep me satisfied. I fed several dollars into a machine that gave me change and started in playing the various pinballs.

I got lucky with a shooting machine, bagging damn near every jungle animal that reared its head over the green-painted metal bushes. But shooting got boring after awhile and I abandoned the machine and got myself a Coke and wandered outside, sipping it, to get closer to the breeze. Before long I found myself staring at the phone booth on the sidewalk in front of the arcade.

Was it too soon to call her? Or maybe too late. I'd been back in Wisconsin four days now, and this was the first time I'd stuck my nose outside my A-frame cottage, other than to swim and fish in the lake that came up to my backyard. Mostly I stayed inside and watched television, listened to my stereo, cooked myself TV dinners. And sat around feeling paranoid.

Boyd had said I was getting paranoid and maybe he was right. Broker was dead and I should've felt fine, nothing to worry about, but I was sitting around like a man expecting a heart attack. I'd even dug out that .38 I'd smuggled back years ago from Nam, and I was carrying it with me all the time, ready to take a potshot at the first thing that moved.

Of course I did have some legitimate cause for concern. Broker had kept me necessarily in the dark about the larger aspects of my work. Perhaps Broker had been some kind of regional manager, reporting back to higher-ups somewhere; if that was true, my name would be known to those higher-ups, of course, and maybe they could put two and two together regarding Broker's demise and come up with me.

And there was that white powder in that little plastic bag. From what I knew of Broker's work, he shouldn't have been involved with that kind of thing. He'd always insisted that he wasn't hooked up to the mob, that we did only piece work for the Family. But suppose Broker *was* directly linked with mob people? Then what? If paranoia is when you think people are out to get you, then are you still paranoid when people *are* out to get you? I mean, shit. It isn't pleasant sitting in a room knowing maybe some stranger's going to walk in off the street with a gun.

The operator told me how much money and I dropped the coins in. I listened to the phone ring and pictured the apartment in my mind and she answered. "Hello?" she said.

I said nothing.

"Hello," she said, "who is this? Hello?"

"Hello, Peg."

"…Quarry?"

"Hello, Peg."

"God. God, Quarry. You're alive."

"How are you, Peg?"

"The papers were full of blood the day after you left. The papers are still talking about it. It's horrible."

"Oh?"

"When Vince turned up dead, I thought…but you couldn't have done that to him. The papers said his body was…you didn't do that to him."

"Peg."

"Yes?"

"It's good to hear your voice."

"It's good to hear…Quarry, people are in town asking questions."

"What sort of people?"

"I don't know. Different sorts. FBI. People like that."

"I see. What sort of questions they asking?"

"I don't know for sure. They haven't talked to me yet. I hope they don't. I don't know what I'm going to say to them if they do."

"Don't say anything."

"You know I won't tell them anything about you. But what about me? My mind's full of what I can't tell anybody."

"Forget all that."

"How can I? Quarry?"

"Yes?"

"Why did you call?"

"I wanted to talk to you. I'd like to see you again, Peg."

"Quarry…"

"Not right away, maybe, but I want to see you. I have some money saved up, Peg. I could help you. Maybe you and I could…"

"Quarry, what are you talking about?"

"Peg."

"I'm just a broad you shacked up with once. For a fucking day, at that. Why talk like it's something else?"

"It is something else."

"How do you know? How do you know you're not just another one-night stand for me, huh? I'm a one-night stand sort of person, you know."

"I feel something for you, Peg."

"Oh, Quarry, goddamn you…"

"I want to see you again."

"I don't know."

"What? You don't know what?"

"I don't know if I want to see you."

"Why?"

"Because I've been thinking, Quarry. I've been thinking about things that happened while you were in town. I've been thinking about certain things you said. I've been thinking about what's been in the papers."

"Forget all that."

"Okay. Okay I will. But first I want you to tell me something. I want you to tell me what you do. What do you do, Quarry? You said you were like Frank. Something illegal. Okay. I can live with that. But be specific. What is it you do, Quarry?"

I kill people.

"You kill people, don't you?" she said.

I said nothing.

"Goodbye, Quarry," she said.

The line went dead.

I played with the shooting machine for another half an hour, and when I quit there were ten free games left on it. Then I went back to my A-frame and for the rest of the afternoon I swam.

Afterword

I began this novel in 1971 when I was studying at the Writers Workshop at the University of Iowa in Iowa City. I was in my last semester, and my mentor, Richard Yates, was no longer teaching there. My current instructor was William Price Fox, the gifted humorist, who was not impressed with my opening chapters, nor were many of the other students in my workshop section (each week the class dissected several stories or chapters by fellow students). Several in class, however, came to my defense and even singled out what I'd done as the best thing they'd seen that year.

Fox and a handful of other instructors who—unlike that fine mainstream fiction writer Yates—had been dismissive of my work suddenly changed their tune, and even claimed me as a prize student, when my first two novels, *Bait Money* and *No Cure for Death*, sold later that same final semester. Only one other writer in the program sold anything professionally that year. (Both my novels were written under Yates' tutelage.)

I was generally considered an eccentric black sheep at the workshop, but having a mentor like Yates offset that. Several other of my instructors also championed me to various degrees, including Gina Berriault and Walter Tevis. But no respectability had been granted by the workshop to genre fiction, and as a budding mystery writer, I had an uphill battle. My thesis was developing three novels that demonstrated crime fiction could be written using a common Midwestern small-town setting (the fictional Port City, based upon my hometown, Muscatine, Iowa, where I still live) rather than the much more common New York or Los Angeles. Regionalism was just around the corner for mystery fiction, but I didn't know that.

The thesis consisted of *Bait Money*, *No Cure for Death* and the unfinished *Quarry*. My memory is fuzzy (not advancing age—it's always been fuzzy) but I believe I set *Quarry* aside to write sequels to the two novels that had already sold. *Quarry* was probably finished by around late 1972 or '73. It did not sell till 1975.

The idea behind Quarry was twofold. I'd already followed my other mentor, Donald E. Westlake, into writing about a thief (*Bait Money* was an homage to his Richard Stark-bylined Parker series, homage being French for "rip-off"). I had trained to write private eye fiction but the times were wrong for that, and also wrong for cop heroes—cops were guys with nightsticks clubbing friends of mine at the '68 Chicago Convention. So the antihero crook was a convenient retreat for a writer who was (as my first agent Knox Burger put it) "a blacksmith in an automotive age."

But I thought Parker and Nolan were to some degree cop-outs. They were "good" bad-guy thieves—oh, sure, hardbitten as hell, but they stole mainly money and only killed other bad guys. In the '60s, banks and the Establishment in general were worthy targets of fantasy revenge.

Also, "Richard Stark" and I both wrote our crook books in the third person. Safe. Detached.

I wanted to take it up a notch—my "hero" would be a hired killer. The books would be in first person. In the opening chapter, Quarry would do something terrible, giving readers an early chance to bail; late in the book he would again do something terrible, to confront readers with just what kind of person they'd been easily identifying with.

And Quarry himself would be somebody like me, just a normal person in his early twenties—not a child of poverty or cursed by a criminal background, but a war-damaged Vietnam veteran. I had a good friend (now deceased) who was very much like Quarry—a sweet, smart, funny guy who had learned to kill people for "Uncle Sugar."

In addition, I wanted to make a comment about Americans in general—that we had, through Vietnam, become numb to death. That we had grown used to watching body bags being loaded onto planes even as we ate our TV dinners taking in the nightly news.

This book, when originally published in 1976 by Berkley Books, was retitled *The Broker*. This was done without my permission or even knowledge. When my character Quarry grew into something of a cult favorite by the 1980s, and I was approached by Foul Play Press to have the first four published in trade paperback, I restored the original title and retitled the other novels too, as they reflected a titling scheme imposed on me—now those Foul Play Press reprints are as rare as the original paperbacks. In the meantime, I started writing about Quarry again, this time for Hard Case Crime, beginning with *The Last Quarry* in 2006, and have so far written seven new Quarry novels for them, with more planned. When Hard Case Crime expressed an interest in the original Quarry novels, I was delighted to have the opportunity to have all the books under one roof.

Quarry apparently is again a cult favorite, in part because Hard Case Crime invited me to write a new novel about him that led to more, as well as a Quarry-derived film (*The Last Lullaby*) and a TV series on the air. But I never forget what Don Westlake told me: "A cult favorite is seven readers short of the author being able to make a living."

MAX ALLAN COLLINS

WANT MORE QUARRY?

Try These Other Quarry Novels From MAX ALLAN COLLINS and HARD CASE CRIME

Quarry's List

When a rival sets out to take over the murder-for-pay business, Quarry finds himself in the crosshairs.

Quarry's Deal

Quarry's plan to target other hitmen for elimination hits a snag when he comes up against a deadly female assassin.

Quarry's Cut

It's not unusual to see bodies on the set of an adult film, but when they're *dead* bodies, Quarry has his work cut out for him.

Quarry's Vote

Happily retired, Quarry turns down a million dollars to assassinate a presidential candidate. But it's not the sort of job you can just walk away from…

Read On for the Opening Chapter of QUARRY'S LIST!

1

A noise woke me.

Not much of a noise, but enough of one to tell me I wasn't alone in the house. The convincing thing was the dead silence that followed that little bump-in-the-night, an unnatural silence, and I found myself holding my breath, much as the intruder downstairs must have been.

I sat up in bed, leaned over toward the window, parted the curtains, and looked out. Looked down. It had snowed today, the season's first snowfall; and the cold late November day had turned into a dark, even colder night. The ground was covered with a good five inches of white, and the footprints showed.

That was when I first consciously realized the .38 was in my hand. I'd been keeping the gun under the pillow on the side of the bed that hadn't been getting much use lately. Neither had the gun, outside of my carrying it around with me all the time, like some sort of goddamn .38-caliber security blanket.

But all blankets were tossed aside now, and I was sitting up in bed, and the gun in my hand wasn't a symbol anymore, not just something to make me feel comfortable. No.

It was something to kill people with.

People like the two men who were invading my lake home at this very moment. Right now there was only one of them in the house, but another man was outside, backing the first guy up. No doubt of that. That was standard, a team of two, but that didn't bother me. They wouldn't be coming in together.

Which was nice, because it's easier to kill people one at a time. Two-on-one may be okay in basketball, but not in this game.

I didn't make any noise getting out of bed. Three and a half months of practice had made me good. The guy downstairs was good, too, I supposed, but he wasn't *that* good; he hadn't lived here like I had, he didn't know this place other than maybe from photographs or an afternoon prowl he and his partner may have made sometime when I was away. And I'm always gone in the afternoon. So it would have been easy.

Easy to get in and look around, yes; but that wouldn't make it easy to invade the place in the middle of an overcast, moonless, colder-than-fuck night. Not without making a noise, anyway.

And, too, I was ready for visitors. Oh, nothing elaborate. No alarm system or any of that bullshit. An alarm system isn't going to do any good if the man who wants to come inside knows what he's doing. Even a good amateur can get around an alarm. And a professional, a thief, say, or a hitman like the one downstairs, wouldn't be stopped by anything but an outrageously elaborate, expensive system with triple backups and the works. I didn't have the money or the patience for that and of course most of the more effective alarm systems are arranged to trigger a light on a panel at some police station, and I didn't exactly want to explain to any police why it was I needed an alarm in my house.

But I did have a system. Not an alarm system; nothing more than my own built-in alarm, which comes from those rice-paddy warfare years I suffered through, where you learned to sleep light unless you didn't care about waking up. The best warning system depends not on electronics, but on devious thinking. You have to be smarter than the guy trying to break in. That comes from Vietnam, too, I guess: the tendency to think of psychological and even guerilla warfare rather than more conventional, unimaginative means.

The layout of my little A-frame cottage is simple: two bedrooms in the rear, one of which is clearly the master bedroom (twice as large as the adjacent spare, and with triple the closet space); a small bathroom next to the master bedroom, across from the laundry room; a big open living-room area, with a kitchenette on the left, as you come into the room from the hallway along which are the bedrooms, bath, and laundry rooms; and an open loft dominated by an oversize couch. The couch converts into a double-size bed at night.

Both bedrooms downstairs have easy-access windows, and the footprints I'd seen had led to both of those windows, so I couldn't be sure which bedroom he'd decided to enter. If my second-guessing of the intruder's strategy was right, he'd have come in the window of the spare bedroom, the one that seemed not to be in use; but he may have been second-guessing me, and might have figured I'd use the spare bedroom to throw him off.

Whichever way he'd used to come in, he was by now surely finding out that the lumpish shape under the covers in the master bedroom's bed was three pillows and not a body. In fact, if I listened real close, I might be able to pinpoint the exact moment when…

And I heard the thud.

I smiled.

There are a number of sounds in the world that can be described by the word "thud," but there is only one sound like the thud that comes from a silenced automatic. And that thud had just sounded in the bedroom downstairs, right below me.

I had him. He was dead. Technically alive, yes, breathing. But dead.

The trick was, since another guy was outside, I probably should kill the one downstairs with his own gun. My .38 was not silenced (as no silencer made can truly silence a revolver, with its exposed chamber) and if I fired it at him, the noise would probably scare away his friend outside.

And I didn't want him scared away.

I wanted him curious.

I wanted him to come in and say hello.

I wondered what the best way would be to get the silenced automatic away from the guy below. I don't like to kill people with my hands; I'm not into that. Strangling people, breaking necks, snapping spines, you can have it.

But it looked like any way I figured it, some sort of struggle was going to be inevitable. Now, I'm not exactly a bruiser; I'm a couple inches under six foot, and at one hundred sixty pounds I was heavier than I'd been in a long time. I'm also no expert in karate or any of that; the only belt I wear holds my pants up. I know the basics of hand-to-hand, from Marine training; but from practical experience I've found that whenever I'm in a kill-or-be-killed situation, pulling a trigger is all the exercise I crave.

On the other hand, there are certain situations where a certain amount of physical violence can't be avoided.

When the guy below me stepped out of the hallway and into the open, I jumped down from the loft and landed with both feet on his shoulders.

The air gushed out of him, but he didn't have a chance to say anything before he was unconscious. He hit the floor limp, like a fat man rolling out of bed, and I came down on top of him, using him to cushion my own fall. The silenced automatic tumbled from his fingers. I picked it up.

A nine-millimeter automatic. Like the one I used to use. I had to smile. The sensation of the nine-millimeter in my hand was not an altogether unpleasant experience. It was almost like shaking hands with an old friend.

On the floor, the guy was starting to rouse.

There were no lights on, of course, so I couldn't see much of him. He was my size, about, a little heavier maybe.

He was wearing black: heavy turtleneck sweater, slacks, even the stocking cap pulled down over his ears. His cheeks were red, against otherwise pale, pale skin.

And now he was up into a sitting position, there on the floor, his eyes open, and before he could say a word I said, "Take off your clothes."

He didn't say, "What?"

He didn't say anything. He was a pro. He just started taking off his clothes, sweater first. The ribbing of thermal underwear was revealed as the sweater gave way. I didn't blame him for the long johns. It was cold out there.

"Just down to your underwear," I said.

He nodded, piled the sweater and slacks and stocking cap on the nearby kitchenette counter. "Shoes and socks, too," I said.

He shrugged and started to unlace his black military-style boots.

"I don't have to tell you not to try throwing a shoe at me or anything, do I? No, I didn't think so."

He put the boots on the counter, and sighed, as if to say, "What now?"

"Back to the bedroom," I said.

He started walking down the hallway. When we got to the end, he veered toward the master bedroom.

"No," I said. "The other one."

I wanted him to use the spare bedroom, because I had new sheets on the other bed, and the bed in here just had some old ragged ones I wouldn't mind messing up. Also, there was a plastic liner.

"Get in," I said, motioning to the bed.

He hesitated, showing confusion and, for the first time, worry.

"Don't screw it up now," I said. "You been fine up to here. Very professional. I respect that. So do as I say, and maybe you'll be around tomorrow. Get in bed."

Reluctantly, he climbed under the covers. There was more light in here, as the drapes were back and the light from the street a quarter-mile over was seeping in. I saw his face: young, rather blank, his features very ordinary but not unpleasant. His skin was extremely pale, the cold-reddened cheeks fading now.

"Pull the covers up around your neck," I said. He did.

"Now what?" he said, speaking for the first time.

And the last.

The silenced nine-millimeter made its thudding sound and I went back out into the living room to get into the dead man's clothes.